*For Richard —
with love*

Roger Stevens

*Roger Stevens*

# CREEPER

**VIKING**

*For Joseph and Judy*

*With special thanks for all her help and assistance to Jill*

VIKING

Published by the Penguin Group
Penguin Books Ltd, 27 Wrights Lane, London w8 5tz, England
Penguin Books USA Inc., 375 Hudson Street, New York, New York 10014, USA
Penguin Books Australia Ltd, Ringwood, Victoria, Australia
Penguin Books Canada Ltd, 10 Alcorn Avenue, Toronto, Ontario, Canada m4v 3b2
Penguin Books (NZ) Ltd, 182–190 Wairau Road, Auckland 10, New Zealand

Penguin Books Ltd, Registered Offices: Harmondsworth, Middlesex, England

First published 1996
1 3 5 7 9 10 8 6 4 2

Copyright © Roger Stevens, 1996

The moral right of the author has been asserted

Set in 13/15pt Garamond Monotype
Set by Datix International Limited, Bungay, Suffolk
Made and printed in England by Clays Ltd, St Ives plc

A CIP catalogue record for this book is available from the British Library

ISBN 0–670–86784–5

The Earth we abuse and the living things we kill
will, in the end, take their revenge,
for in exploiting their presence we are
diminishing our future.

Marya Mannes *More in Anger* (1958)

# CONTENTS

# CHAPTER I

# THE BLACK MOTH

*Joe came in from school, his boots heavy with mud — so heavy he could hardly lift his feet. He tossed his school-bag across the room and chuckled as his books spun out in slow motion, spilling on the floor. He turned on the TV. There was an old black-and-white war film on. Boring, Joe thought and changed the channel. Same thing — the old war film. Weird. He tried another station. That film again. Every channel he tried was showing the same film. Tiger Moth biplanes were fighting the Germans, wheeling in smoky grey circles around the grainy grey skies.*

*As Joe stood there, one of the planes flew out of the television screen into the room and started buzzing round his head. At that moment the telephone rang in the kitchen and Joe could hear his parents having a row. His dad appeared, the phone in his hand. The Tiger Moth made a bee-line for his father, firing its tiny guns at him, tracer arcing around the room.*

*'Watch out!' Joe yelled, but it was too late.*

*His father burst into a ball of violet flame. Joe tried to get up, to go to his father, but he couldn't: he was stuck. The mud on his boots was sticking fast to the floor. He made one last superhuman effort and heaved himself towards his dad . . .*

I

Joe opened his eyes and stared up into the darkness of his bedroom. His heart was pounding and he was wet with sweat. He could hear the telephone ringing in his mum's bedroom. It stopped in mid-ring. That's what woke me, Joe thought, the phone. Still feeling shaky from the nightmare, Joe groped in the darkness for the switch and turned on his bedside lamp, blinking in the sharp brightness. He could hear his mum talking in a low voice in her bedroom. He peered at the clock. Just after midnight. He felt as though he'd been asleep much longer than that. He snuggled down beneath the warm duvet, listening to the desolate wind as it swept in across the marsh from the distant sea, and the rain, still hammering against his window.

What a weird dream. But Joe knew about dreams. He knew they were usually prompted by something in real life, and he knew that this one came from the worry in his mind about his dad. And from his plans for tomorrow.

Joe had been angry and upset when his dad hadn't turned up yesterday. His dad had promised to be back in time. He'd been away for two weeks now but he had absolutely *promised* to take Joe fishing yesterday morning. His dad had never let him down before. As the day wore on Joe's anger had turned to worry. He'd thought about the things that had happened in the last couple of weeks. His mum had been in an odd mood lately. She was either very cheerful, more cheerful than usual, or else depressed, bursting into floods of tears at the silliest things, like when he walked mud in all over the kitchen floor. Well, he could sympathize – she *had* just spent half an hour cleaning it. But bursting into tears? He'd asked her what was wrong, of course, but all she said was 'Nothing,' and then cried some more. If his dad had been there he'd have given her a cuddle and winked, and it would have been all right. But his dad was away.

Joe's dad had explained the special project on the marsh, and said he would be away for a week or so. He was a scientist working for the water company and spent most of his time on the marsh – checking water-levels, inspecting and repairing dikes, monitoring wildlife, that sort of thing. But before he'd gone he'd promised Joe that he'd be back by the first Saturday of half-term, and they'd spend the day fishing. Well, that had been yesterday – and he hadn't turned up. Surely he couldn't have forgotten. No, of course not.

Joe had got to thinking then. It was so unlike his dad. What if he was out on the marsh injured? What if he was caught in some animal trap or had fallen into a ditch? Two weeks was a long time. What sort of special project took two weeks? Surely he'd be back by now. Joe had said as much to Mum but she'd smiled sadly and replied, 'Don't be silly. He'll be back any time now.' Then she'd given him a big hug. That wasn't like her, either, giving him a big hug when it wasn't bedtime. So he'd devised a plan. In the morning he was going to get up early and go out on to the marsh to search for his father.

As he lay there thinking, wondering where his father could be, Joe heard another sound, a faint buzzing, and his ears pricked. Fragments of the nightmare about the tiny war-plane fleetingly returned. Suddenly a huge black moth flew towards the bedside lamp, its dark shadow flashing before it across the wall and ceiling. The moth settled on the lampshade, fanning its big, black wings.

Joe stared at it. It was nearly as big as his hand and it looked quite eerie with the bright light shining through it. The light made it look transparent, like a ghost. He had never seen a moth like it – and he knew all about moths. Studying wildlife was one of his hobbies. He took after his dad in that respect. Looking after the environment was more than just a job to Joe's dad. He loved being outdoors, learning about everything that grew and lived on the marsh. And particularly he liked watching birds. He'd always take his binoculars with him when he was working.

Joe decided to look the moth up in one of the many reference books that filled his bookcases and shelves and spread out in a jumble over the floor. Quickly he slipped out of bed, shivering as a cold draught of air from the open window blew against his naked skin.

He turned in time to see the moth. It had left the lamp and was flying straight at him. Joe ducked in alarm, feeling the cold breath of its wings on his cheek. But he knew moths weren't dangerous. The sudden light has probably disoriented it, he thought. The moth flew at him again, more gently, and this time settled on his arm. Joe studied it, fascinated. Moths usually steered clear of people. But this was too large to be any usual variety. Closer inspection revealed a white mark on its head, in the shape of a human skull. Wow! A death's head hawk-moth. He'd never seen a live one before and this beauty had actually settled on his arm. Joe studied it carefully. Funny. He thought the death's head moth was much smaller than this. And this one had black wings. Usually the death's head was pictured as yellow with brown stripes. This must be a rare variation, thought Joe.

4

Then the moth bit him. Joe yelled in pain. It felt as though a row of tiny burning needles had been jabbed into his arm. Tears came to his eyes. He slapped at the moth but the black insect was already buzzing through the air, circling Joe's head. Joe ducked and dived, slapping the air uselessly with his hands. The moth flew behind him, but before Joe could turn to face this new attack, it settled on his back. He could feel its tiny cold feet crawling up his skin, sending little shivers up his spine, but whichever way he twisted his body he couldn't reach it. At any moment it could bite him again.

Slowly, so as not to unsettle it, Joe sat down on the bedroom floor and gradually eased his body backwards, at the last moment hitting the floor with a thump. The moth tried to fly out of the way but couldn't escape the weight of his body. He felt it squidge beneath him as he wriggled against the carpet. Satisfied that it had to be dead, he rose unsteadily to his feet. His arm was beginning to hurt where the moth had bitten him. A red blister had already formed. Gingerly he picked the squashed insect up with his thumb and finger and stared at it. He didn't like killing things.

'It was you or me,' he said apologetically.

'You OK?' he heard his mum call.

'I'm all right,' he called back. 'Just stubbed my toe. I'm going downstairs for a glass of water.'

He ought to tell his mum about the moth, he knew. He wasn't sure why he hadn't, except that it would be one more thing for her to worry about.

Delicately Joe placed the dead moth on his bedside table and headed downstairs to the bathroom to put some cream on the bite. He'd never known a moth bite anyone before.

Back in his room, Joe hunted through his mess of books and at last found the one he wanted. From the warmth of his bed, he thumbed through his *Comprehensive Illustrated Guide to the Moths and Butterflies of Britain and Europe*. The death's head hawk-moth was certainly the nearest to the one that had attacked him. He was pleased to see that he'd been right about the death's head's colouring – yellow with brown stripes. But nowhere in the book could he find a reference to moths attacking people. He inspected his arm: the blister looked red and angry. The cream had soothed it a bit but it still hurt. Well, if it was still bad in the morning he'd show his mum. Carefully he picked the dead insect up and laid it in the back of the book, closing it gently. He laid the book on the floor. He'd have a proper look tomorrow. Joe turned out the light.

Snuggled down beneath his duvet, Joe lay in the dark and thought about the next morning. Earlier that evening he had packed himself some sandwiches and crisps, as well as some tins of soup and beans and a small Calor-gas burner. He'd packed his tent and sleeping bag into his rucksack, along with a spare T-shirt and spare socks, cleaned his fishing-rod again and checked the bait and set his alarm for half-past five. When the sun came up he would be out on the marsh, fishing. Or at least, that was his cover story. Really, he was going to find his father. He hadn't told his mum that or she would have stopped him. She'd taken a while to agree to him even going fishing on his own.

Joe hoped his dad wasn't hurt. The marsh was a dangerous place. Anyone would tell you. No one went there – at least, not unless they had to. Farmers grazed sheep there and fishermen fished the Three Lakes, but no one went right into the marsh, not into the wild parts. For one thing, a large part of it was behind a high, barbed-wire fence where the army used to have a firing-range years ago. There were still notices everywhere, warning people to keep out.

There were all sorts of tales told about the marsh. There were stories of weird creatures that lived beyond the fence, monsters who would creep into the town at night and steal boys and girls and spirit them away. Joe remembered hearing only that week of a girl who'd disappeared. The word round the school was that she'd been snatched by the marsh creatures. He didn't believe it, of course. Nobody really believed it, but some people did think the marsh was haunted. Joe didn't believe that, either. There was always a rational explanation for ghosts, he thought. But there were dangers on the marsh, natural ones, and he was determined to find his dad.

As sleep finally came, Joe thought he heard his mother sobbing in the next room.

## CHAPTER 2

# A NEW FRIEND

In the morning Joe was up very early, even though it had been hard to drag himself from the warmth of his bed. Downstairs, he spread some golden syrup on his toast, nice and thick so it dribbled on to his fingers, drank some Coke and hurriedly gathered his gear together. He made a flask of tea and did a final check that he hadn't forgotten anything. He'd put a nice thick jumper on under his coat to keep warm – if today was like yesterday he'd need it. Then he wrote a note to his mum: 'I've taken my tent. If the fishing's good I might camp the night.' She wouldn't be pleased, but at least he'd let her know. He called a whispered goodbye up the stairs – he didn't want her to wake up – and left the house as quietly as he could.

The morning was icy cold and his breath turned to plumes of steam in the air. The rain had stopped but the October sky was overcast. Joe knew that somewhere above the clouds the sun was rising, but on the ground it was still dark. Joe took one last look back at his house and set off at a fast pace. A brisk ten-minute walk through the outskirts of the small town, its wet streets strewn with fallen leaves, and Joe had reached the deserted road that wound round the edge of the marsh.

He said good-morning to a milkman who muttered something about the morning being miserable and then ignored him. So much for milkmen being cheerful, Joe thought. The sky was a little brighter now and the dawn chorus had begun its shrill cacophony, welcoming the day. Funny, Joe thought, birds never complain about the weather. The dawn chorus happens every morning whether it's sunny or rainy, hot or cold. People could learn a lot from birds.

Joe greeted an old couple being pulled along by a huge black-and-tan Labrador. They smiled and wished him a good-morning. That's more like it, he thought. Other than those early risers, he seemed to have the world to himself.

Joe followed the muddy car track that led to the lakes. He should have worn his boots, he realized. He'd have been able to stomp straight through the puddles. As he skirted the mud, trying to keep to the firmer ground between the parallel tyre tracks, he thought about what he was doing, where he was going. A gate barred his way. A notice proclaimed *Private fishing. Permit holders only.*

Joe climbed the gate and balanced on the top bar, wobbling slightly. He gazed out on to the vast, gloomy wilderness stretching before him, a dull green emptiness relieved only by a few stunted trees and bushes that lined the dikes. Patches of mist moved slowly across the distant landscape and the wind moaned softly. The marsh was a spooky place and it was easy to see why superstitious people thought it was haunted.

Somewhere in the far, far distance was the sea, but the horizon was a blur of misty greyness. And somewhere out there, perhaps, was his dad, lying helpless in a bog or with his foot caught in an animal trap. The marsh is so big, Joe thought, suddenly overcome with doubt. How on earth did he expect to find his father out there? It was a stupid idea.

A shaft of sunlight escaped through a break in the cloud and picked out a lone gull, wheeling high overhead, in a splash of gold. The gull let out a long wail, like a baby crying for its lost mother. Almost immediately the cry faded into the desolate emptiness before him. Somewhere a sheep bleated in reply and then the marsh was again still. At once Joe felt terribly alone.

'Hi, there!'

Somebody was calling him.

Joe looked anxiously about. Who else would be out here at this time of the morning? A ghost? Of course not. A fellow fisherman? No, it was a girl's voice.

Joe looked round. She was running awkwardly along the pitted track towards him. She had a pale face with almond-shaped eyes and tangled black hair. She wore a tatty coat and mud-splattered blue jeans and looked bedraggled, as though she'd been up all night and hadn't slept. Joe guessed she was about his age, a bit smaller than he was maybe – but who was she? He climbed down from the gate to meet her.

'Hello,' she said, out of breath.

'Hi,' Joe replied, wondering who she was and what she wanted.

There was an awkward silence.

'I know you, don't I?' the girl finally said. 'I've seen you at school.'

'Probably,' Joe said, but he didn't recognize her. He felt annoyed. He didn't have time to stop and chat with girls. But what did she want? Why had she run to catch him up?

'My name's Hannah. What's yours?'

'Joe.'

'Oh yes, of course,' she said. 'Where are you off to?'

Joe thought it looked obvious. After all, he had a fishing-rod tied to his rucksack, even if it was in its case.

'Fishing,' he said. 'What about you?'

'Oh, you know – just out for a walk.'

'Do you normally go for walks this early in the morning?' Joe asked, surprised.

Hannah nodded. 'All the time. Do you mind if I come along with you? I've never been fishing.'

Joe did mind. Having a girl follow him about was the last thing he wanted. But he couldn't just say no, could he? 'Well, it's quite a way, where I'm going,' he said. 'I'm going to be camping the night, too. Your mum and dad will wonder where you are.'

'That's OK. I don't have to stay all day, do I?'

What could he say to put her off? he wondered. 'But then you'd have to come back across the marsh on your own. It's dangerous.'

'No it's not.'

It *is* dangerous, Joe thought. He was allowed to go to the Three Lakes to fish but he wasn't allowed into the marsh proper on his own. And there were always stories on the telly about children being taken away by strange men in cars. For a moment he wondered if this was the girl who'd disappeared. But he dismissed the thought. This girl hadn't disappeared. She was here.

'Can I come, then?' Hannah asked.

Joe sighed. It meant he would have to tell her why he was really here. But maybe not. She'd probably get bored before they'd even reached the fishing lakes, before she realized he had no intention of fishing. But then again – did it really matter if she knew anyway? It was only a secret from his mum, so she wouldn't worry. It might be better to have someone to talk to. She seemed friendly, after all, and none of his mates need know he'd spent the day with a girl.

'You can come if you want,' he said, and swung himself over the gate with what he hoped would be an impressive acrobatic leap. Instead he landed with a squelch in a muddy puddle and for a moment had to struggle to keep his balance.

'Great,' Hannah laughed and climbed over after him.

They walked for twenty minutes or so, neither saying very much. Joe strode briskly along in front, secretly hoping Hannah would tire and leave him alone, but she kept up without complaining. In fact she seemed to be lasting better than he was. She had a spring in her step, while he was already beginning to feel weary – and it was still really early, too early to be tired. Joe increased his pace. He'd show her.

It was properly light now but the weather was still cold and miserable. The sun had made no more appearances. They passed by the first two lakes, devoid of fishermen this morning, as though the weather was too miserable and gloomy even for them.

At last the track they were following petered out into a car-park that gave access to the last and largest of the lakes. They crossed the muddy ground to a stile where Joe called a halt for a rest. Beyond the stile some old railway sleepers crossed a dike and a narrow footpath led into the marsh proper. To the right and left a wooden fence followed the dike as far as they could see. Joe surveyed the landscape ahead. It looked much wilder than the marsh they had crossed so far and he could just make out the high fence put up by the Ministry of Defence long ago to protect their land. The dike and the fence with its stile were a boundary: this was where the real marsh started. Go no further, the land seemed to say. Ahead lies danger. Ahead there are things that you really wouldn't want to know about.

A chill, drizzly breeze blew into their faces.

'When are you going to start fishing, then?' Hannah asked.

Joe was about to tell her the real purpose of his journey when he spotted something hanging on the fence to their right. It was a large, green canvas bag. Joe felt his heart thumping in his chest. He couldn't be sure, of course, but it resembled his father's.

'Look,' Joe said excitedly, pointing.

'It's a bag of some kind,' Hannah replied and shrugged. 'So what?

'I think it might be my dad's holdall.'

Hannah gave him a strange look. 'Your dad's holdall? What on earth would that be doing here?'

The ground around the edge of the car-park was soft and muddy and overgrown. Brambles covered the fence.

Joe picked his way carefully through the thistles and grasses towards the bag, his feet sliding on the wet, slippery vegetation. He managed to keep his balance, though, and, leaning forward, he grabbed the wooden fence stake, letting it take his weight. With one hand he strained to reach for the holdall.

Something in the bag moved.

## CHAPTER 3

# A CLUE

J oe jumped back in alarm, nearly losing his footing.
'What's up?' Hannah called.

'The bag. It moved. I think there's something in it.'

'It was probably the wind moving it.'

Joe stared at the bag. Was it his imagination? There *was*
quite a wind. The fence was swaying slightly. Slowly he
leant forward again and grasped the handles of the holdall, awkwardly unhooking it from the fence with one hand,
gritting his teeth as the brambles scratched him. He made
his way back to Hannah by the stile. He was sure he could
feel something inside the bag moving.

'Is it your dad's?' Hannah asked.

'I'm not sure.' Joe laid the holdall carefully on the
ground and regarded it uncertainly.

'Open it, then,' Hannah said.

'What if there's something inside it? A trapped animal,
I mean.'

'Don't be silly,' Hannah said, and she bent down and
unzipped it. 'There's clothing of some kind, I think.' She
pulled out an old, waxed coat.

Joe grabbed it and unfolded it, holding it up. 'It might be Dad's. He does wear a coat like this when he's working on the marsh.' He draped the coat over the stile and picked the bag up again. Then he screamed and jumped back, throwing the bag to the ground. A white head with two tiny pink eyes poked out.

'A rat,' Hannah said, unfazed.

'Made me jump,' Joe stammered. 'It's a big one, isn't it?'

The rat hissed at them and bared its tiny, pointed teeth. It stared at them for a few moments then began scrambling out of the holdall. Joe retreated several more steps. The rat's fur was pure white but grew in tufts, revealing red-raw patches of skin. You'd have felt sorry for it but for the angry, piercing stare from those bloodshot eyes and the hissing smile. This was nobody's pet.

'Stay still,' Hannah said. 'If you don't do anything it will probably leave us alone.'

'I'm not so sure,' Joe murmured.

They stared at the rat for a few moments. 'It's mangy,' Joe whispered, 'and it's going bald.'

Hannah nodded. The obese rat stared back at them with its evil pink eyes, as if deciding whether to attack or not. For a moment the wind dropped and the marsh grew silent, as though holding its breath.

Agonizing seconds passed as the rat and the children looked at one another, as though each were waiting for the other to make a move. Joe could hardly bear it. Then, all at once, the rat turned and ran, under the stile, across the bridge, and disappeared from view into the undergrowth beyond.

Joe stood for several empty seconds staring at the

holdall, as if expecting more rats to jump out at any moment. Then he breathed a sigh of relief.

'I'm sweating,' Joe whispered. 'Are there any more in there, do you think?'

Cautiously Hannah crept forward and turned the bag on its side with her foot. 'I don't think so.'

Joe took his rucksack off and unclipped his fishing-rod. He poked around inside the bag but nothing happened.

'I think that was the only one,' he said.

Hannah picked up the bag, turned it upside-down and shook it. Pieces of paper fluttered out and a notebook dropped to the ground.

'Quick,' Joe yelled. 'Catch them.'

For a few minutes they rushed around, chasing the pages fluttering in the breeze, slipping and sliding about. Hannah was giggling which made Joe cross. It took a while but at last they'd rounded them all up and put them back in the bag for safety.

'This looks a bit like Dad's notebook,' Joe said. 'He keeps one for jotting down things he has to remember when he gets back. Stuff like that. It's a bit of a mess, though. It's been chewed up.'

Carefully he turned over the few pages left in the book.

'Look, a drawing of a crested lark.' He gazed at it for a few moments, thinking of his father. Joe couldn't recall his dad drawing pictures but that didn't mean it *wasn't* his dad's.

Hannah was looking perplexed. 'But I still don't understand what it's doing here.'

'Well,' Joe said, 'you see . . .' He looked at the stile, as though expecting the rat to return any minute. Hannah was looking at him, waiting. He'd have to tell her what he was really doing here – but what if she laughed at him? Still, he had no choice, he realized, not if he was to carry on with his search. He took a deep breath.

'Er . . . you see, I didn't really come here to fish. My dad's late.' This wasn't going very well. He tried again. 'Dad often works on the marsh. But this time he's been gone two weeks and he hasn't come back yet. He was due back yesterday and he was going to take me fishing. I thought I'd go and find him. I thought that if I, you know, hunted around, I might find a clue of some kind about where he was.'

Hannah thought for a few moments, frowning. 'Is that a clue, do you think?'

'I don't know,' Joe said. He felt relieved. She seemed to be taking him seriously. 'Maybe.'

He went through the scraps in the bag. 'This is all illegible. The rat must have chewed it up. No, I don't think it's his.'

'But you think your dad might be out here somewhere, then?'

Joe nodded. 'I'm sure of it.'

Hannah pulled a face. 'It's a bit unlikely, though. I mean, if your mum was worried she'd have called the police, wouldn't she? And if he is out here – how will you find him? I mean, the marsh is huge. You'd never find a body out here on your own. You'd need tracker dogs and all sorts, I mean . . . oh.' Hannah had just realized what she'd said.

Joe was staring at her, a look of horror on his face. Hannah had said a *body*. The thought had been there all the time in the back of his mind, and now Hannah had said it. But his dad couldn't be dead, could he?

Hannah put her hand on Joe's arm. 'I didn't mean . . . Look, I'm sure he's not dead or anything. He could just be lost.'

'No,' Joe said. 'He knows the marsh. He'd never get lost. But he could be trapped somewhere.'

'So, what are we going to do now?' Hannah asked. 'Go and look for him?'

Joe climbed the stile. He stood on the top, the wind ruffling his hair, and looked out over the wilderness beyond. What was he going to do? His father was out there somewhere – waiting to be rescued. He turned to look at Hannah. He liked her, he realized, but did he really want her to come with him?

'Yeah. I'm going to look for him,' Joe said.

'I can come, can't I?' Hannah asked. 'I've not got anything else to do. It'll be good for you to have some company.'

Why not? Joe thought. 'OK,' he said gruffly. 'Let's go.'

They crossed the stile and made their way along the path.

Behind them the mangy rat peered out from beneath a clump of spiky thistles, watching them, its eyes bright and intelligent. It turned and ran, along small, secret pathways, overtaking them, as silent as a passing shadow.

They walked for what seemed like hours, following the narrow, twisty, overgrown path. In places it disappeared altogether beneath dog rose and nettle and they had to make detours to find it again, getting wet, scratched and

19

stung in the process. And still the rain drizzled and the chill breeze blew.

Suddenly the path forked. The left-hand fork seemed to lead round and back in the direction from which they had come, while the right led to the high fence, the boundary of the Ministry's land.

'Which way?' Joe asked.

'I think we should go that way,' Hannah said, indicating the path that led towards the fence.

'I'm not sure,' Joe said doubtfully.

'Well, the other path looks like it goes back the way we came. Your dad wouldn't have gone in a big circle, would he?'

Joe wasn't sure. It was equally unlikely he would have gone on beyond the fence and on to the army's land. He'd often told Joe to keep away from there.

'We could at least take a look,' Hannah urged.

There didn't seem to be any harm in just looking, Joe figured.

'OK,' he said. 'We'll take a look.'

The path to the fence was very overgrown. It led to a small gate. The heavy padlock was rusted and a big notice, its letters faded by the sun and rain, proclaimed, *DANGER. KEEP OUT*. In smaller letters it said, *Army firing-range. Authorized personnel only. Strictly private*. Somebody had graffitied the sign and added a B in front of the A of Army.

Joe smiled and then sighed.

'That's it, then,' he said. 'Dad couldn't have come this way.'

They stared at the fence for a few moments.

'What's that?' Hannah exclaimed. She walked along the edge of the fence. 'Look.'

Joe followed her. A big hole had been cut in the thick wire meshing. 'Maybe your dad went through that?'

Joe stared at the hole. He examined the cut ends of wire. They weren't rusty, as he would have expected. The hole must have been made quite recently.

'But why would he have gone in there?' Joe asked.

'It would explain why he's missing, wouldn't it?' Hannah replied. 'You said he'd been gone two weeks. He'd have been found by now if something had happened to him near the lakes.'

The picture of his dad stepping on an old unexploded mine flashed into Joe's head. He tried not to think about it. Perhaps she was right. It would explain his dad's disappearance.

'But why would he have gone in there in the first place?'

'I don't know. I've just got a feeling about it. Come on.'

Hannah squeezed through the hole.

'We'll have to be careful,' Joe said. 'We'll have to watch where we're walking. There might be live ammunition lying about.'

'No, it's quite safe.'

'But we're not allowed in there. And how do we know it's safe?' Joe asked.

'Well, the path is sure to be safe, isn't it? Hurry up,' Hannah said, and started walking.

Well, it did make some kind of sense, Joe thought. And it wouldn't hurt to look. He crawled through after her and rushed to catch her up.

## CHAPTER 4

# WASP

They followed the path for some time, the fence disappearing from view behind them. The path seemed to be leading them to higher ground. Hawthorn bushes covered in bright red berries now lined the route and they had to pick their way through masses of brambles as the path wound up the side of a small, rocky hill. The ground levelled out at the top and they found themselves in a clearing, scattered with rocks, with a clear view of the marsh ahead. Joe felt cold and wet and tired. He was looking forward to his lunch.

'There's quite a view from up here, isn't there?' Hannah said. 'It gives you a strange kind of feeling. As though we were the only two people left alive in the world.'

Joe unslung his rucksack and dumped it on the ground. The two of them gazed across the marsh. It stretched as far as the eye could see, disappearing in a dark, misty blur on the horizon. Gulls wheeled overhead, crying forlornly in the wind. Leaves chased around the bushes and brambles that grew over the rocks.

'Can you hear them? Voices in the wind – talking to us?'

Joe chuckled 'Ghostly voices? You're not worried about the marsh being haunted, are you?'

'Of course not,' Hannah said. 'But it's so big and so . . . well, lonely. And frightening. Surely you feel it? You must.'

'I don't think it's frightening,' Joe said. 'I like it. Dad used to bring me on to the marsh. Not this bit, though. We saw some rare birds, not just gulls. There are lapwings, plovers, birds you see nowhere else. Bird-watching used to be one of my hobbies. Now I like anything to do with wildlife and nature. I'm going to be a naturalist when I grow up.'

'It's a very scary place,' Hannah said softly to herself, as though lost in her own thoughts.

As Hannah stared across the marsh, Joe rummaged in his rucksack and produced a small stove which he placed carefully on a patch of even ground. Then he found his tin plate and special all-in-one camper's knife, fork and spoon set. Finally he produced a tin of baked beans. Hannah watched as he opened the can and lit the burner. 'We'll have to share the plate, I'm afraid. I didn't know I'd have company.'

'Look at that wasp,' Hannah said in a quiet voice. 'That's frightening. I bet you've never seen one like that.'

Joe laughed. The rat had scared him, but wasps he could cope with. 'You're not afraid of wasps, are you? I . . .' Then Joe saw it. It was no ordinary wasp. It was the size of a matchbox.

He jumped to his feet in alarm. They stared at the wasp as it buzzed around the tin of beans, now bubbling on the stove.

'It's big, isn't it?' Hannah said. The wasp landed on the

hot rim of the can and took off immediately, its feet burnt. It buzzed noisily and angrily around the stove.

Big's not the word, Joe thought, looking desperately around for something to hit it with. The giant wasp darted at him and he tried to duck out of the way, but he wasn't quick enough. The wasp settled on his nose. Joe froze, his heart beating wildly. Can it smell fear? he wondered. He could feel its tiny legs as it walked up his nose, and see the blur of its face and flickering antennae as it neared his eyes. What now? Stay still. Don't antagonize it. His mother's words from the distant past came back to him. It will only sting you if it's frightened. It's got no reason to be frightened of me, he thought. I'm the one that's scared.

The wasp buzzed into the air and settled on Hannah's arm. Joe grabbed a stick lying near by and swiped at the insect, knocking it to the ground. Then he trod on it, smearing its body in a bloody green trail across the earth with the toe of his trainer. They both stared at its remains.

'Why did you do that?' Hannah asked, puzzled. 'I thought you liked wildlife. You just said you wanted to be a naturalist.'

'But it was going to sting you.'

'I don't think so. It wasn't attacking us. It's not the wasp's fault it was so big.'

'What do you mean?'

For a moment she stared at Joe, then smiled a lopsided smile. 'Are you OK?'

Joe was shivering. 'A bit shaken, I suppose. I hope there's not a nest of them near by,' he said nervously.

'I doubt it,' Hannah said. 'Perhaps it's a queen, looking for somewhere to nest for the winter.'

'Maybe,' Joe said. 'It could have been a hornet. They're bigger than wasps. But I've never seen one that big. Perhaps we should move on. Or go back.'

'I'm starving,' Hannah replied. 'Let's eat first.'

After some hot baked beans, a cheese sandwich and some tea from his flask, Joe felt a little better.

'Maybe we *should* go back,' he said.

Hannah shook her head. 'No, we can't give up yet. We've only just started looking! Let's go on. We'll have plenty of time to get back before it gets dark. If we really want to.'

Joe started collecting his bits and pieces together. 'OK, if you're sure you still want to come along.' He thought for a moment. 'But we're not really going to find anything, are we?'

'You're a funny boy,' Hannah said. 'You plan this expedition, pack everything you'll need. You've only been travelling for a few hours but already you're talking about going back. I'd never go back if there was something I had to do.'

Joe looked at Hannah quizzically. 'What do you mean, "If there was something you had to do"?'

There was a strange look of intensity on Hannah's face.

'You know . . .' She seemed to be searching for the right words. Then she appeared to relax. 'Well, like finding your dad. It's important, isn't it?'

'But there's something odd going on,' Joe said.

Hannah stood up and brushed the crumbs from her coat. 'That doesn't mean we should give up. We've hardly started yet and there's a long way to go.'

'I suppose you're right.' Joe sighed. 'Come on, then.

There's a river ahead. Must be the Dence. I can wash the things there. We'll decide then if we want to go on.'

'OK,' Hannah agreed.

'In the mean time,' Joe said, 'how about some chocolate?' He fished out half a bar of Dairy Milk from his pocket. 'I've been saving this.'

Hannah's eyes lit up. 'Yes, please!'

CHAPTER 5

# SEED DISPERSAL

It took an hour or so to reach the River Dence. The path was wet and muddy and the drizzle had turned to rain. The river was further away than it had looked from the top of the hill and the going was slow. The water was high, swelled by the heavy rains of the last few weeks. Thick reeds grew along its banks and huge dragon-flies darted and danced above the water's surface, the metallic blues and mauves of their bodies flashing in the light reflected from the water. Joe watched them warily, the attack by the wasp still fresh in his mind. Once at the river, he rinsed the meal things and, wiping them with a tissue from his pocket, stowed them back in his rucksack. A dilapidated wooden bridge spanned the river.

'Well, we haven't met any more giant wasps,' Hannah said brightly. 'And we've forgotten all about old mines, haven't we? Shall we go on, then? You said you've got a tent. It'll be fun. I've never camped out in a tent before.'

'Really?' Joe was amazed to hear this. 'I've only got one sleeping-bag, though. And it will be cold.'

'I don't feel the cold. Anyway, I'm enjoying myself.'

'You are?' Joe was surprised. He felt wet, cold and miserable and was still not convinced they should continue. But she was right: they hadn't stepped on any unexploded mines, or caught sight of anything to do with the army, nothing exciting like a rusty tank. The army had probably cleared all that sort of stuff up long ago. Well, they'd go on then and if Hannah got freezing cold in the middle of the night, he'd be able to say I told you so.

'Aren't you?' Hannah asked, interrupting his train of thought.

'Aren't I what?'

'Enjoying yourself.'

'Oh, what? Er, yes, of course,' he said, not quite able to admit that he wasn't.

'And look, it's stopped raining. That's a good sign, isn't it? I'll lead the way, shall I?'

Before Joe could say any more, Hannah set off, walking with a light step along the muddy path. Joe followed her wearily. If it wasn't for the fact that he might find his father he would *definitely* have turned back. Not for the first time he wondered what had possessed him to undertake such a silly journey. What did he hope to achieve? But, despite the weather, it was good to be on the marsh. Hannah was right. Maybe he should simply enjoy it. It was an adventure after all.

'Wait for me,' he called.

The rat scrambled on to the bridge from its hiding-place and preened itself as it watched the two of them walk deeper into the marsh.

Progress became even more difficult. The landscape

seemed much wilder than before and the path was becoming much harder to see amidst the dense undergrowth of nettles and thistles. Their progress was frequently interrupted by dikes filled with stagnant muddy water and tall reeds and each time they had to find a route across them. This meant picking their way along one bank until they could find a place clear enough to jump across. Then they would have to go back along the opposite side until they found the path again. Ahead of them was another hill, a possible campsite, but despite their efforts to go forward it seemed to be getting no nearer.

'Look at that,' Hannah called over her shoulder. 'Isn't it pretty? It looks like a party balloon, doesn't it?'

Here the path had widened and the ground was relatively clear. The balloon was drifting towards them in the breeze. Joe caught Hannah up and they watched its lazy journey towards them.

'It looks like a huge seed-pod of some kind,' Joe said. It was a pale straw colour and wisps of grass-like material hung beneath it like string. It was hovering now, just off the path, bobbing gently up and down in a pocket of disturbed air.

'I'll try and catch it,' Joe said.

'No,' Hannah yelled. But Joe was already off the path, reaching for it. A gust of wind blew it a little further away towards a stumpy hawthorn bush. 'Leave it,' Hannah cried.

Joe turned towards her and laughed. 'Don't be silly,' he said. 'I can get it easily.'

At that moment the seed-pod brushed against the bush and there was a loud explosion. Sharp thorns shot in every direction. Instinctively Joe ducked, but he squealed in pain as several of the thorns hit him, piercing his clothes and burying themselves in his skin. Joe jumped back on to the path and sat down, tears in his eyes.

'What happened?' he moaned.

'It's OK,' Hannah said soothingly. 'That must be its way of dispersing seeds I think. Let's have a look at you.'

Hannah inspected Joe's back and carefully pulled out one of the thorns. Joe winced in pain.

'It's a good job you were looking at me when it exploded,' she said. 'If one of those thorns had hit you in the face . . .'

'I've never seen anything like that before,' Joe said, wiping away a tear with the back of his hand. 'My back feels like it's on fire.'

Hannah found three more thorns and pulled them out.

'I don't remember the marsh being like this before,' Joe muttered, standing slowly. 'Giant wasps, exploding seedpods. What's going on?'

Hannah shrugged. 'You OK now?'

'Yes, I'll be all right. My back hurts though.'

'I'll have a proper look later,' Hannah said. She gave his hand a squeeze to reassure him. Joe pulled away.

'Did you bring any first-aid stuff? You'll probably need some cream or something where those thorn things went in,' said Hannah.

Joe shook his head. 'I didn't think about that.'

Hannah tut-tutted reprovingly. 'Come on, let's get a move on. It's getting late and it will be getting dark soon. Look, we're nearly at the hill. You can show me how to pitch a tent.'

'All right,' Joe said. 'We'll build a fire and have supper. I'm starving. I'd feel a lot better if I could get warm and eat.'

'Cheer up,' Hannah said. 'Have the last bit of your chocolate.'

'Thanks,' Joe said glumly.

As they set off for the hill Joe glanced back at the empty seed-pod, hanging from the bush. Like a deflated balloon now, after a birthday party. But this expedition was no party. In the morning, he decided, he was going home, Dad or no Dad. He'd had enough of this adventure already.

CHAPTER 6

# BLACKBERRIES

It took another two hours to reach the hill. Two hours of negotiating dikes, clambering around great clumps of bramble and skirting huge areas of nettles which grew above their heads. There were thistles, too, and a spiky plant that neither Joe nor Hannah recognized but which they gave a wide berth after the incident with the seed-pod.

At one point they had to retrace their steps when their way was blocked by a colony of huge red ants which were busy dragging a dead mouse along the path. As they approached, the ants suddenly turned to attack them, swarming over their feet. They ran, hopping and slapping at the ants which clung to their shoes, until they were some distance away, at which point the ants seemed suddenly to lose interest, and dropped to the ground and disappeared.

Joe's legs ached and his back felt stiff. Every step he took irritated his sore skin. Hannah, on the other hand, seemed unaffected by the day's march. She was as bright and as cheerful as when Joe had first met her that morning. Her constant smile was beginning to irritate him, too. Nobody could be that happy all of the time.

The path they had been following went around the hill and they had to find a route that would take them to the top without having to wade through the nettles, thistles and brambles which grew in profusion around the lower slopes. Here the brambles were covered with huge, ripe blackberries. Joe tried one. They were delicious – fat, juicy and sweet.

'Be careful with those,' Hannah said.

'I know, I know,' Joe replied. 'Deadly nightshade grows near blackberries. But these are definitely blackberries.' He picked some more and ate them. 'Try some. They're delicious.' He gave one to Hannah and she looked at it suspiciously. 'Try it,' Joe said.

Hannah popped it in her mouth.

'Good, eh?'

Hannah smiled and nodded and picked some for herself. 'They are delicious,' she said.

Joe wiped away the juice that was dribbling down his chin with the back of his hand and looked around for a way up the hill.

'There,' he said. 'Let's try this way.'

Once through the dense undergrowth it became much easier. The hill was quite steep in places, but as they climbed the brambles and nettles gave way to bushes and scrub which in turn gave way to silver birches. Huge rocks of grey granite seemed to grow from the ground which was covered in a layer of red and golden leaves. It all seemed somehow out of place, as though they were no longer on the marsh but in some distant woodland.

They reached the top, a plateau dominated by a gigantic

finger of red and brown granite that pointed accusingly at the darkening sky.

Painfully Joe unslung his rucksack and walked across to Hannah who had her ear pressed against the giant monolith. What on earth was she up to?

'Hear anything?' Joe asked her sarcastically. 'More voices?'

'The secrets of the marsh,' she whispered, and gave him a peculiar smile, her bright eyes looking straight through him. Joe turned away.

'Not really,' she added, and laughed lightly. She ran her palm along the rock face, stroking its damp, smooth surface. 'Impressive though, isn't it?'

Joe nodded. It *was* impressive, reaching up into the sky, dwarfing them both, but he refused to appear impressed in front of Hannah. 'Some geological freak, I think,' he said knowingly. 'There shouldn't be any granite around here, of course. It's all chalk and limestone.' Joe didn't know if that was actually true, but it sounded good.

But what was he doing, trying to impress Hannah, as if he was an expert or something, trying to make her feel small? This stupid expedition was his fault after all, and she had tried to warn him about the seed-pod. He was just getting tired.

'Come on,' he said, his voice softer. 'I'll let you help me put up the tent.'

'Thanks,' Hannah said and smiled sweetly.

It was nearly dark by the time they had the tent up. Hannah had obviously enjoyed herself, bashing in the tent-pegs with the mallet. They stood back, slightly out of breath, to admire their achievement. The ground in the shadow of the mighty rock was flat and fairly soft. The tent was small, with a built-in groundsheet, but big enough to hold the two of them. Joe pulled out his sleeping-bag. He threw it into the entrance and bundled his rucksack in after it.

He looked around. As campsites went, it was pretty good. The tall rock would protect them from the wind and he could just make out a river, probably the Dence again, winding around the bottom of the hill. That would be handy for drinking water and washing. Now all they had to do was build a fire.

They were searching in the gathering gloom among the wet trees, hoping to find some dry wood and twigs, when they heard barking, followed by a whimpering noise.

'Sounds like a dog,' Hannah said. 'It's in trouble, I think. Maybe it's caught in a trap or something.'

Joe had visions of a giant dog, the size of a haystack, lying in wait to pounce on them. But he dismissed it. A moth that bites, a giant wasp – but surely not a giant dog?

'This way,' Hannah whispered.

'Be careful,' Joe whispered back.

Cautiously they made their way through the copse of trees, following the sounds made by the dog. Angry barks and snarls were interspersed with frightened whining sounds. They found themselves in a clearing where two huge rocks formed a natural alcove. In the alcove was the dog, a Border collie, its teeth bared, its body shaking with fear. Standing before the dog was a large, white, furry rabbit.

'The dog's caught a rabbit,' Joe whispered.

'No,' Hannah whispered, 'I think it's the other way round.'

The rabbit turned to face them. Its wild, red eyes stared at them. It opened its mouth to show off its rows of sharp teeth and two huge fangs and it let out a long, low, angry snarl.

# CHAPTER 7

# JUDY

Joe and Hannah stood and stared. The white rabbit was snarling at the Border collie, inching nearer all the time. So intent was it on its victim that, although it had stared straight at them, it hadn't registered their presence. The dog was whimpering, growling, barking, shaking. It glanced up and saw Joe and Hannah for the first time.

*Noise! Make a noise. Shout! Yell! Do something! Help me. Please.*

'What was that? Voices? Did you hear them?' Joe said, turning to Hannah. Suddenly he felt scared. The voices were in his head.

*Noise! Just make a noise. Quickly!*

'The voice. There it is again,' he gasped. By now the rabbit, like some nasty overwound clockwork monster, was nearly upon the dog, and about to explode in a shower of teeth and spit and blood, about to tear into the terrified animal.

*Help me. For goodness' sake! Shout or something!*

'Only one voice,' Hannah said quickly. 'I hear it. It's coming from the dog.'

Joe looked at Hannah incredulously. 'You must be joking.'

'No I'm not,' Hannah said and she suddenly started jumping wildly up and down, yelling and waving her arms. Slowly the rabbit turned to face them, fixing them with an evil stare. Its teeth were bared and spittle was dribbling from its fangs.

That's done it now, Joe thought. At once the dog threw back its head and started howling. Joe decided he'd better join in the cacophony.

'Whaaaaahhhh,' he shouted at the rabbit. 'Clear off. Get away. Get out of here.'

He, too, started jumping up and down.

The rabbit spat at them and hissed. Its fur bristled and Joe thought it was about to attack – but all at once it turned and bolted, disappearing through the silver birch leaves and brambles.

'Wow!' Joe said. He realized he was shaking.

The dog ran straight across to them, still trembling, but with its tail wagging like a windmill.

Joe and Hannah both reached down to stroke it.

*Thanks.*

Joe recoiled. A telepathic dog? Surely not.

*Bit of a tight spot, that, eh? A tight spot, eh? Glad you could make it. Glad indeed, oh yes, oh yes.*

Hannah crouched down and flung her arms around the dog.

'There, there,' she cooed. 'It's all right. The nasty rabbit's gone now.' The dog licked her face and she laughed with delight. 'What's your name?'

*Judy. Judy Heregirl. Thank you. That was a tight spot, wasn't it?*

'Yes, it was, Judy,' Hannah said. 'Is that your name? Judy Heregirl?'

*Yes, yes.* Judy licked Hannah's face some more. Hannah giggled.

Joe was staring at the two of them, open-mouthed.

'I'm dreaming, aren't I? Tell me this is all a dream.'

Joe hadn't yet decided whether he believed in God or not, but he looked up at the sky and shouted at the clouds. 'It is a dream, isn't it? Tell me it is.'

'I don't think so,' Hannah said. 'Judy can communicate with us in our minds.'

Joe shook his head in disbelief. 'But it's impossible.'

Hannah shrugged. 'It can't be impossible because it's happening. I think you'll just have to accept it.'

Joe crouched down and stroked the dog.

'I'm Joe,' he said, 'and this is Hannah.' What did he think he was doing? Introducing himself to a telepathic dog?

The dog started licking Joe's face, too. *Pleased to meet you. That was a tight spot, wasn't it?*

'It certainly was,' Joe said. He stood up. What was happening here? This wasn't the marsh he'd visited before with his dad. This wasn't the marsh where they used to fish for newts and watch for hours to catch a glimpse of a lapwing or a partridge. It was all wrong. And the rabbit. A ferocious rabbit that attacked dogs? He glanced around nervously. Whatever would attack them next? In the morning he was definitely going home. This place was dangerous. It was more than dangerous. Then he had an idea. He stroked the Border collie's black-and-white head.

'We're looking for someone,' he said.

Was he just as crazy as this place, Joe wondered, asking a dog questions?

*Yes, looking for someone. Who might that be, then?*

Joe described his father and explained how he might be lost on the marsh or trapped somewhere.

*I did see someone. Might have been your father. Near the sea, it was. I'm going the other way. I'm going to find civ . . . civ . . .*

'Civilization?'

*That's it. People. It's not good here. Very bad place for a dog.*

Joe felt elated. A real clue. If the dog was right . . .

'Could you take us there?' Joe asked.

*Where? Civ . . . away from here?*

'No, to the sea, of course. To find my dad.'

*Oh, I see. Well, OK. Of course I can. I owe you one.*

Joe wondered where the dog had learned English. It sounded like she must have watched a lot of television when she was a puppy.

Hannah stood up and glanced at the blackening sky. 'We'd better get this kindling collected and get back to the tent. We won't be able to see soon. It's nearly dark.'

For a moment Joe had been ready to continue their journey, but Hannah was right. They wouldn't get very far at night. They'd need the fire, too – a big one to keep any unwelcome visitors away. Who knew what other surprises the marsh might hold? And he was cold.

Somewhere in the distance they heard the low rumble of thunder. As if on cue it started to pour with rain. That's all we need, Joe thought.

## CHAPTER 8

# STORM

Joe lay in the tent, listening to the heavy, uneven beat of the rain on the material. What a day this had been. He still couldn't make any sense of it. Giant wasps, killer rabbits and now a telepathic dog. Lighting a fire had proved impossible. The wood they'd collected had been too wet to burn and once the rain had started, it didn't stop. His back was sore from the flying thorns and he was freezing cold.

He was excited at the prospect of finding his father. Judy had seen someone and it might be him. But Joe felt scared. What if something terrible *had* happened to him? He didn't want to think about that. Anyway, his father had probably only been delayed. He wouldn't be pleased that Joe had crossed the marsh. His dad might even be at home now, in the warm, watching the telly. Or having a row. His mum and dad seemed to be rowing a lot lately.

Searching for his dad had seemed to Joe like a good idea in the cosy comfort of his home, but things had certainly not turned out the way he'd expected. They'd eaten the rest of the food, too. They really ought to turn around and go back in the morning or they would starve. He'd brought enough food for a couple of days but he hadn't been expecting to share it with anyone.

It was crowded in the tent. Hannah was snuggled up between him and Judy, the dog, to keep as warm as possible. It was cold now – but it would be freezing in the early hours. Still, Hannah hadn't complained. Maybe he should have let her have the sleeping-bag. Then again, it had been her choice to camp with him. Why should he get cold?

'Hannah,' he whispered. 'You OK?'

'Hmmmmm?'

'Hannah.'

'Hmmm?'

'Hannah – you asleep?'

'I *was*,' she whispered back.

'I was thinking. Won't your parents be worried where you are?'

Hannah yawned and Joe could feel her stretch beside him. 'Oh, they're both away for a few days.'

Joe listened to the wind and rain some more. 'You sure?'

'Look . . . I'd rather be here than all on my own at home.'

'But surely the neighbours or someone will be round to check you're all right.'

'No. We live miles from anywhere. My parents often leave me on my own. It's OK.'

It all sounded a bit odd to Joe. Her parents often left her on her own? Well, it wasn't his problem, was it? Obviously her parents were nothing like his mum and dad.

After a few moments Hannah said, 'Can I go back to sleep now?'

'Sorry. I couldn't sleep, that's all.'

'OK. And don't worry. We'll find him tomorrow – safe and sound.'

'I hope so. Good-night, then,' he whispered.

'Good-night.'

*Good-night.*


Joe awoke with a start. He'd been dreaming about snakes. Huge, long, twisty snakes, chasing him through cold, wet leaves that clung to his muddy shoes, slowing him down. He'd heard his dad calling to him somewhere ahead, but his father was nowhere to be seen. Then Joe had slid in a patch of mud and fallen and the snakes had begun to crawl all over his body. He had felt their ribs moving beneath the smooth skin.

Joe felt sick. He had pains in his stomach. Indigestion. He must have eaten something that disagreed with him. He lay in the darkness waiting for the sick feeling to go away. He hoped he wasn't going to *be* sick. He didn't want to go outside. The wind was howling now, even louder than before, and the rain was drumming furiously on the tent. If he went outside he'd get soaked.

He could feel Hannah's warmth beside him and hear her breathing, slow and regular. Judy was making soft whimpering noises. She's dreaming, too, he thought. Dogs usually dreamed about chasing rabbits. Judy's dream was probably the other way round.

He could feel the tent moving as the wind gusted around them. There was quite a storm out there, but the little tent was standing up to it well. He hoped they'd put the tent-pegs in properly. If the tent blew away they would be in trouble. But there was nothing he could do about that now. He just hoped that it would hold.

Joe raised himself up on his elbows and stared into the darkness, at the dim shapes of his new friends, sleeping soundly. Suddenly he noticed two pink dots in the corner of the tent. He blinked. They looked like eyes, small, burning, animal eyes. He felt his heartbeat quicken and a knot tie itself in the pit of his stomach. What was it? He screwed his eyes up tight and opened them again. The eyes had gone. Had he imagined them? Was something there? What if the creature, whatever it was, got into his sleeping-bag?

Joe snuggled back down, pulling the sleeping-bag tightly around him, and listened, straining his ears for any tell-tale sounds. He could hear his companions breathing and the gale howling outside, but no furtive scrabblings from the intruder. But what was that? No, he must be mistaken – only the tent poles creaking in the wind.

The ground felt hard and he turned over, trying to get comfortable. His back itched. Sleep, he must get back to sleep. Everything would be all right in the morning. There was certain to be a logical explanation for all that had happened today. Sleep. He curled up in the cosiness of the sleeping-bag. If only he didn't feel ill. He tried to forget the sick feeling. Sleep. He yawned. Of course there couldn't be an animal in the tent, Judy would have seen it off. Imagination. Had Judy really communicated with them? No, of course not. He'd imagined that, too. Imagination. Logical explanation. That's right. He heard his mum's voice in the wind. Sleep tight. Mind the bedbugs don't bite.

Joe woke up and shivered. Mum must have forgotten to put the heating on. He would have a big fry-up for breakfast this morning. Three eggs, sausages, fried bread and a huge plateful of baked beans. He was ravenous. For some reason his bed seemed unusually hard. He opened his eyes and stretched. His body ached and his legs and arms felt stiff.

He peered over the top of his sleeping-bag and remembered. He was camping, of course. He sat up and looked round. No sign of Hannah or the dog. Keeping his balance as best he could in the tiny space of the tent, he pulled his jeans on and his jumper over his head. Then he pulled on his trainers. He was busting for a pee. Wonder where the others are, he thought.

He was so hungry, but the idea he'd had of a big breakfast disappeared as he remembered they'd eaten all the food. Plenty of tea, though. Luckily he'd thought to bring tea-bags and powdered milk. He remembered the nearby stream. There'd be water, too. He'd make a big flask of tea for later.

Joe emerged from the tent, blinking into dazzling daylight. The sky was a brilliant blue, not a cloud to be seen and, despite the early morning chill, out of the tent he could feel the warmth of the sun on his face. Joe looked around. The huge pointed rock behind the tent was shimmering in a blaze of sunlit colours – deep browns and ochres and sandy reds. He looked at the tent, pleased that it had weathered the storm. The dew-soaked grass around his feet was a rich green, glistening in the sunshine, and there was no sign of the carpet of autumn leaves that had littered the ground the day before. The gale in the night must have blown them away. Perhaps today would be all right after all.

He saw Hannah sitting on a rock at the edge of the hill, staring out at the marsh. He went for a pee behind the huge granite finger and then he joined her.

As he looked around his brief optimism crumbled. There would certainly be plenty of water to make the tea. The marsh was flooded. It looked like a gigantic lake. No sign of dry land in any direction, just water, water and more water, sparkling in the morning sun.

They were marooned.

Joe sighed. No food and now we're stranded on a hill in the middle of a flood. He looked around for Judy.

'Isn't it beautiful?' Hannah said.

'Great,' Joe replied. 'But what do we do now?'

'I'd like just to stay here. Just us and Judy, not having to go back to the mountain. It's so peaceful. How did you sleep?'

'OK, I suppose.' What did she mean – go back to the mountain?

'It was fun, wasn't it, sleeping in a tent?'

'Oh yeah,' Joe said, his voice sounded more sarcastic than he'd meant it to. 'What mountain?' he asked.

Hannah suddenly stood up. 'Where's Judy?'

Yes, where was she? Joe had heard barking just now. He looked around and called her.

'Judy? Judy?'

There was a rustling from the nearby bushes and Judy

came bounding towards them, a stick in her mouth. She dropped the stick and jumped up, resting her wet paws on his chest, her tail wagging furiously. He grabbed her, laughing, and ruffled her shaggy hair.

'Good girl, Judy,' he said. 'You know what? I had an odd dream about you. I dreamed that you could talk to me!'

*What's so odd about that?*

It was true, then. He stroked her head and sighed.

'Nothing,' he said. He bent down and picked up the stick. 'You want me to throw this?'

*Yes, please. Throw it. Go on. Throw it.*

Joe hurled it into the trees and watched Judy chase down the hill after it.

'You know what,' Joe told Hannah, 'Judy may be able to talk to us but I don't think she's very bright.'

Hannah smiled. 'It's what dogs do, though, isn't it? They chase sticks. How about a cup of tea, then?'

'Just what I was going to suggest,' Joe said.

'I'll have mine without that powdered milk if that's OK?'

'Sure,' Joe said. Judy reappeared with the stick and dropped it at his feet. 'Oh dear. This could go on all day, couldn't it?'

*Yes, please.*

Joe and Hannah sat together on the large flat rock that overlooked the flooded marsh and sipped their tea. The tea tasted wonderful. Joe had packed the tent up and they were almost ready to go. But where and how? That was the next problem. Judy was busy gnawing at the stick.

'We could swim,' suggested Hannah.

*Swim. Yes, go for a swim.*

'I don't think so.' Joe glanced up at the sky. Not a cloud to be seen. But how long will it last? he wondered. It will probably cloud over again by lunch-time and then there'll be more rain, he thought gloomily. That won't help the water go down. His gaze roamed around the island. Trees. There were lots of trees. Perhaps they could build a boat. No, that would take for ever.

'We could build a boat,' Hannah said.

'That's a stupid idea,' Joe retorted. 'It would take for ever.'

'I'm sorry,' Hannah said, slightly hurt, 'it was only a suggestion.'

They sat in silence staring at the flood water. Somehow Joe couldn't imagine that his father was out there. He made a decision. When the water went down they would go back.

'What's that?' Hannah asked.

'What?'

'Over there,' she said, pointing. 'It looks like a big boat. That's good, isn't it? Now we won't have to build one. I wonder if they can see us?'

Hannah stood on the rock and started waving frantic-ally. Judy started barking. Joe shielded his eyes and fol-lowed Hannah's gaze. Ah, there it was. She was right. There was a boat and it seemed to be coming in their direction. They were being rescued. Someone must have seen them heading for the marsh and sent out a search party. His mum must have been worried in the storm and realized what had happened. Joe jumped to his feet and joined in the waving and shouting. The boat had changed direction slightly and was now coming directly towards them. Someone on board was waving back.

'Come on,' he said excitedly to Hannah and Judy, 'they've seen us.'

Joe grabbed his rucksack and they scrambled down the rocky hillside. The boat was drifting closer now, trailing a black shadow across the sparkling water, heading for the overhang of rock. It was a big old barge with a tall mast and dark brown sail. It looked as though it had seen better days. It edged as close as it could to the rock and a wooden gangplank was thrown down for them to climb aboard.

Hannah jumped on to the gangplank, almost lost her balance, regained it, and ran aboard, helped by eager hands. Judy followed.

'Come on,' Hannah yelled at Joe.

But Joe was standing frozen to the spot. Biting moths, giant wasps, telepathic dogs – they were nothing to what he saw waiting for them on the boat. Well, it was crazy, Joe figured, but there was nothing else to do but accept it. As Hannah had said, the impossible wasn't impossible if it was actually happening. Carefully he made his way along the swaying wooden plank.

From the bank a rat, its patchy fur wet with dew, watched the children board the barge. It sniffed at the water apprehensively, it nose twitching, its pink eyes sly and bright. It slipped into the water and began to swim.

## CHAPTER 9

# STREAK

J oe stood on the deck and looked awkwardly around. Monkeys. He was surrounded by them. There were monkeys on the cabin roof. Monkeys climbing the big brown sail. Monkeys shuffling all around them, chattering excitedly. But they seemed friendly and Joe relaxed a little. Hannah had a big grin on her face and Judy was wagging her tail, but, even so, Joe noticed, the monkeys seemed to be giving her and the dog a wide berth and kept glancing nervously in their direction.

The monkeys were about half Joe's height, furry brown with white faces. Cute and cuddly, Joe thought. But then he noticed that many of them had arms missing. In fact, he saw they were all missing the same arm – the left. No stump, either, just a missing arm. The deformed ones seemed older than the other monkeys, their hair speckled with silver grey. Cute and cuddly? There was the smell, too. It was like the monkey house in the zoo.

One of the two-armed monkeys stepped forward.

'Welcome aboard,' he said in a high squeaky voice.

So, talking monkeys. Joe wasn't really surprised. He felt

as though his surprise muscles had all been used up. At least the monkeys didn't seem hostile.

'Er . . . thank you,' Joe said. 'Um . . . my name's Joe and these are my friends, Hannah and Judy the dog.'

The monkey showed his yellow teeth in a grin and bowed. Joe bowed back.

The monkey bowed again. Joe was wondering whether *he* should bow again when the monkey spoke.

'They call me Streak,' the monkey said.

Joe saw that he had a streak of white fur that zigzagged across his chest.

Joe held out his hand and was for some reason reminded of Stanley meeting Doctor Livingstone in the jungle. The monkey scratched under his arm. He couldn't imagine Doctor Livingstone doing that.

Joe wondered what to do next. They were all looking at him, even Hannah and Judy.

'Where are you going?' he asked.

'Yes, yes,' the monkey said excitedly. 'Where are we going?'

Joe was confused. 'Yes, where?'

'Where are we going?' the monkey repeated. He waved his arms around his head. 'Here and there.'

'Where?'

'Here and there. Wherever the river takes us.' The monkey spun round and clapped his hands. 'Stow the main brace. Lift up the sails. All decks to hand. Monkeys away.'

All the monkeys started running around, chattering wildly. Two of them moved the gangplank and another pulled up the anchor and Joe felt the barge sway and begin to move slowly from the shore.

'Come on,' Streak said, 'I'll show you round.' And without waiting he scampered off. Joe, followed by Hannah and Judy, hurried after him.

Joe and Hannah sat on a wooden crate at the prow of the large sailing barge, watching the flood water glide beneath them. Occasionally they drifted by an island of rocks and scrubby bushes. It was hot, more like a summer's day than October. Joe had discarded his jacket and thick jumper. He had no idea what was going on, but he had no choice but to go along with whatever happened, talking dogs and sailing monkeys and all.

He was eating boiled fish. Very tasty, although it was a specimen of fish that Joe didn't recognize. For some reason it reminded him of strawberries. The monkeys, who had caught the fish, ate them raw, but Joe had cooked some for him and Hannah on the little camping stove. Judy was nowhere to be seen. The monkeys had overcome their initial fear of the dog and Judy was enjoying herself, giving them rides around the deck on her back.

Joe threw the remains of his fish over the side, licked his fingers and wiped them on his sleeve. 'That fish. It had an amazing taste. Well, what are we going to do now?'

'We're going to find your dad.'

'I've been thinking about that. I don't think he's here. He wouldn't have come on to the army's land. And even if he did, what chance have we got of finding him? The marsh is huge. I think we should go home.'

'We can't,' Hannah cried.

'Of course we can. The water's already going down. We'll probably run aground soon. Haven't you noticed?

There are more and more islands and bushes and stuff sticking out of the water. These marshes have all those dikes running through them. That's what the dikes are for – to drain the water away.'

Hannah sniffed and turned away, peering ahead. 'Well, I didn't think you'd give up so soon.'

'Maybe not, but as soon as we can get ashore, that's what I intend to do. It was a stupid idea, thinking my father was trapped on the marsh.' Joe began packing the stove away. He was thinking how lucky it was that he'd brought all his camping gear when he suddenly realized something.

'Oh no,' he said.

'What?'

'I've left my fishing-rod and the tent back on the hill. In the rush to get rescued. I just didn't think. Dad bought me that rod. He'll kill me if I lose it.'

'Don't worry,' Hannah said, 'I expect it will still be there when we come back.'

'I suppose so.'

Well, it would be safe enough for the time being. At least he'd picked up the sleeping-bag and the rest of the stuff.

Joe turned around and watched the monkeys sitting in little groups on the cabin and the deck. At first they'd seemed very lively, just as you'd expect them to be. Now they seemed more listless, tired even. Especially the one-armed monkeys. There was no sign of Judy. He hoped she was all right. No sign of Streak, either.

'You noticed anything?' Joe asked.

'No, what?'

'The monkeys – they seem to be identical.'

'Of course they are.'

'No. I don't mean similar – I mean absolutely identical. All the one-armed monkeys have the same arm missing. And they're just . . . well, just . . . *so* alike.'

'Streak isn't.'

'Well, no, he isn't. But all the others are. I mean cats are alike, aren't they? But you'd recognize your own. And Judy. If she was in an identity parade with a load of other Border collies, you'd be able to pick her out, wouldn't you? But these monkeys . . . it's as though they were two sets of identical twins. Well, not twins exactly . . . You know what I mean.'

'Except for Streak.'

'Except for Streak,' Joe conceded.

'Ahoy there, me lovely hearties,' a voice shrilled from somewhere above them. They looked up. It was Streak with a couple of other monkeys, waving at them from the top of the sail. 'Come up here, shipmates.'

Hannah grinned.

'See me climbing up there,' Joe muttered.

Streak clambered down the sail, landed lightly at their feet, and scratched himself.

'We're back on course,' he said. 'We've found the river.'

'Great,' Joe said. 'Where *are* we going?'

'Up the river, of course.'

'But don't you have somewhere to go? Where do you come from? Don't you want to go home?'

Joe was wondering if the monkeys had escaped from a circus or a zoo, maybe.

Streak began to fidget uncomfortably.

'This barge is our home. We don't want to go back. Not to the mountain . . .'

Suddenly there was a loud shrieking from the top of the sail.

Streak glanced up. 'All hands on deck. Prepare to repel boarders. All hands on deck,' he yelled.

The monkeys sprang into activity, rushing up to the barge's rails. More monkeys appeared from below. Weapons were being passed around – metal pipes, wooden clubs, even a garden fork.

'What is it?' Joe asked. He and Hannah peered into the water. Joe couldn't see anyone attacking them.

Judy came bounding up, barking.

*A fight, a fight. We're going to have a scrap.*

The monkeys were making a deafening din.

'Look!' Hannah pointed. The water around the barge was beginning to froth and bubble. There were things swimming in it, churning it up. They could see flashes of white.

'Rats.' Joe yelled. 'Thousands of them!'

CHAPTER 10

# RAT ATTACK

The first rats swarmed over the side of the barge, their eyes bright with hatred and their teeth bared. More rats followed and then more, clambering over the wooden rails, scrabbling along the wooden deck, trailing water from their wet fur. At once the monkeys were upon them, beating them with their rusty pipes, clubs and sticks, with whatever weapon had come to hand.

Judy was barking, attacking in a frenzy, snarling and biting. She grabbed a squealing rat by the neck and tossed it overboard. Then another and another.

Joe and Hannah were backing away. Joe felt sick and afraid – the squashed rats, the blood and the guts, it was too much for him. At first the fight seemed very one-sided – the rats, squeaking and spitting, were being knocked back into the water or squashed. But not for long. As fast as the rats were killed or thrown overboard, more were appearing to replace them, until the rats outnumbered the monkeys. Still more rats came pouring over the side of the barge; there were more now than the crew could cope with. Monkeys were being bitten, too. They were rushing about, swinging wildly with their makeshift weapons, screaming and jabbering.

'The rats,' Joe yelled at Hannah. 'Look. They all look like the rat that was in that holdall. They've all got patches of fur missing.'

'I know,' Hannah yelled back, over the din. 'But don't worry, the monkeys will see them off.'

Joe stared at her. She looked so calm while he felt terrified.

Streak squealed as a rat leapt at him and attached itself to his arm with its razor-sharp teeth, sinking them into his fur. A monkey wielding a large, rusty spanner rushed to Streak's aid and swung at the rat, knocking it to the floor with a thud. Unfortunately the spanner also connected with Streak's head. Streak yelped in pain and toppled over.

The one-armed monkeys were suffering particularly badly. The rats were winning the fight. There were just too many of them for the monkeys to cope with. Several monkeys were lying on the deck, whimpering and moaning, as the mass of white, wet bodies trailing long, thick, fleshy tails crawled over them. Judy was picking squealing rats up and throwing them in all directions as fast as she could, but it was a losing battle.

The rats didn't attack Joe or Hannah, though, but gradually they gathered around them in increasing numbers, forcing them back against the edge of the cabin, hissing at them.

'Look,' Joe gasped, pointing.

A rat, twice as big as the others, its white fur tufted and spotted with black, was heaving its great fat body over the rail. It balanced on the top, staring at Joe and Hannah. All at once the other rats stopped, became still, their vicious blood-pink eyes fixed on the huge, mottled monster. All went quiet. The monkeys stopped and stared.

'What now?' Joe whispered in alarm.

As if by some predetermined arrangement, all the rats began to move slowly in Joe's and Hannah's direction. They would have to make a run for it, Joe thought. But how? Now they were surrounded and the rats were closing in. Joe could feel panic welling up inside.

Suddenly Judy dived at the great rat, taking it by surprise. Before it had time to react, she had it by the throat. The rat screamed, an agonized high-pitched wail.

A shudder ran through the other rats as they watched Judy hold the rat high in the air and drop its writhing body over the side, back into the river below. In unison all the rats scrambled madly for the side of the barge and dived for the water. Within seconds they were gone. Judy's tail was wagging furiously and she was growling and barking with delight.

The last rat to desert the barge perched on the rail, looking directly at Joe and Hannah, fixing them with its pink eyes. Then it, too, was gone.

Joe let out a long sigh of relief and the monkeys started yelling and cheering. They descended on Judy, patting her and hugging her and leaping around her in a crazy dance. The monkeys who were lying on the deck pulled themselves slowly up, inspecting their injuries, dazed and sore, but jubilant. Streak, holding his head, made his way across to Judy.

'Well done, me shipmate, you saved the day,' Streak said.

*It was nothing. Nothing at all. I saw them off. I had that rat's number. Oh yes, I had him. Nothing at all. Easy. Easy.*

'Come on,' Hannah said to Joe. 'Some of the monkeys look in a bad way. We'd better see what we can do. Pity we don't have a first-aid kit.'

'All right, all right,' Joe said sharply. 'I'm sorry I forgot to bring one.'

Joe was still shaking. He stood still for a few moments and let himself calm down.

'I'm sorry,' he said.

There was no point being nasty to Hannah. She was right. The injured monkeys needed help. Then he had an idea. 'Perhaps there's a first-aid kit on this barge. I'll go and see.'

Joe climbed down the ladder and reappeared after a couple of minutes.

'It stinks down there,' he said, screwing up his face, 'but I've found it. A first-aid kit. Bandages – all sorts of stuff. They're a bit grubby, but they'll do.'

Hannah was staring into the distance, at the misty blur of the horizon. She turned and smiled at Joe, sadly.

'Well done. Come on, then. Let's get to work.'

They began patching up the monkeys. Joe inspected Streak's head. The spanner had cut the skin but the wound didn't look too deep. 'You'll be all right,' he said. 'Tell you what, I've got an idea.' He rummaged in his rucksack and brought out his spare T-shirt. He began to rip it up.

'What are you doing?' Hannah wanted to know.

Carefully Joe folded a strip of the red T-shirt and wound it round Streak's head, tying it, and letting the loose ends dangle at the back. 'There,' he said. 'Now you look like a pirate.'

'A pirate, eh?' said Streak. 'Well, timber me shivers.'

They both laughed.

The red sun was low and the sky was shot with delicate pinks and purples. Joe's fears that they would have more rain had proved to be unfounded and the flood water had subsided. Joe and Hannah were perched on the cabin roof, finishing their supper, more boiled fish. Joe was getting bored with it. Judy was sleeping on the deck below. It had been a baking hot day, more like summer than late autumn, and Joe and Hannah were down to their T-shirts. The crew were sitting around listlessly, nursing their bites and bruises, as the barge continued its course along the river.

'I've been thinking,' Joe said, 'about what I said earlier. In the morning I'm definitely going ashore. Then I'm going home.'

'Giving up?'

'If you like,' Joe said. Hannah was beginning to annoy him. He should have gone earlier, after the attack by the rats.

They both watched the river bank sliding lazily by, each wrapped in their own thoughts.

'Hannah,' Joe said after a while, 'where do you think these monkeys come from? It's been puzzling me all day. Do you think they escaped from a zoo or a circus?'

'That's probably it,' Hannah said.

Joe picked the last morsels of flesh from his fish and looked around.

'And I don't see how they can talk, either. I saw a

programme on the telly once about how intelligent chimps are. They trained a chimp to understand human speech – but they couldn't get it to talk because chimps don't have the right vocal cords. It must be the same for monkeys, so how can these monkeys talk?'

'Well, they can, can't they?'

Hannah was infuriating. Here was a mystery, probably a scientific breakthrough, and Hannah didn't seem in the least bit interested in solving it. She seemed to be taking everything so calmly. Joe licked his fingers and gathered together the remains of the meal.

'I'm going to find Streak. I'll ask him. Maybe he can throw some light on it.'

Hannah was lying down, her eyes closed. Joe climbed down to the deck.

'I'll see you later.'

'OK,' Hannah muttered. She opened her eyes and sat up, watching Joe as he walked across the deck.

Joe found Streak at the bow, gazing into the gathering gloom. He seemed fed up, not his usual cheery self.

'It's no good,' Streak said, scratching himself under his arm. 'I tried to tell 'em. They wouldn't listen. Monkeys aren't really very bright, you know.'

'What's up?'

The monkey looked up at him with his big brown eyes and began scratching vigorously under his other arm. Joe found himself scratching too. Whenever he talked to the monkey he started to itch. Streak looked up at him sadly and reached for Joe's hand. It was an odd sensation, holding a monkey's hand. It was so small and warm, like a young child's.

'It'll be OK, though, won't it?' Streak asked softly. 'You'll help us. You won't let it get us, will you?'

Joe nodded, not quite sure what the monkey was talking about.

Streak stared ahead. 'We're going the wrong way. Going back to the mountain. Somehow we must have turned around.'

'The mountain?' There was something nagging at Joe. Something Hannah had said. He was about to question Streak about the mountain when the monkey suddenly pulled his hand away.

'Oh no,' he said, alarmed. 'I hope that's not what I think it is.'

'What?' Joe asked, peered into the failing light. Streak was becoming agitated. They seemed to be heading towards a black cloud that had settled on the water some way ahead.

Streak started shrieking. 'Change course. Turn around. All hands on deck. Change course.'

Joe could see the black cloud clearly now as the barge moved towards it and he fancied he could hear a high-pitched buzzing sound. For a moment he was reminded of the moth that had bitten him in his bedroom. The cloud was huge, much bigger than the barge, and it seemed to be alive. What was more, it was moving, too, and heading straight for them.

## CHAPTER II

# OWLS

Before Joe had the time to try and work out what to do, the barge was already nosing into the swirling black cloud. The edges of the cloud were fuzzy and indistinct, and the high-pitched buzzing was getting louder. Joe looked around desperately for some means of escape. He could see Hannah climbing down the side of the cabin. Monkeys were rushing about as Streak continued to yell instructions, but everything was confused and there was no time to think.

Mosquitoes buzzed around Joe's face. He slapped them away. They were huge – the size of crane-flies. Of course! That's what the cloud was – mosquitoes. And they were sailing straight into it. All at once it was dark as the barge entered the insect cloud, a buzzing maelstrom of mosquitoes. It was as though the light of the setting sun had suddenly been turned out. Already the excited insects were settling on Joe, on his face, his neck, his hands – wherever his skin was exposed. The high-pitched buzzing noise blotted out all the other sounds. He felt as though he was being choked. Wildly he waved his arms, trying to brush them away, but it was useless.

The blurred bodies of shrieking monkeys bumped into Joe, nearly knocking him over.

'Hannah,' he shouted desperately over the noise, 'Hannah!'

But he heard no answer. Joe began to panic. There was only one way out.

Joe ran to where the side of the barge must be, slapping at the sharp stabbing pains on his face and arms, feeling for the rail. Without any hesitation he jumped. He hit the water in a shock of freezing spray – but the buzzing stopped instantly. Joe felt the cold, dark water drawing him down. He kicked his legs, propelling himself away from the side of the barge, and thrust towards the surface. But the current held him, its invisible hands holding him under, pulling him down. He kicked harder but it was no good, the current had a grip on him. He let it take him for a few seconds, swimming with it, then kicked out again, by now desperate for oxygen, his lungs aching, and at last his head broke the surface and he took a big gulp of air.

Joe trod water, looking anxiously around for the barge. It was nowhere to be seen. He suddenly felt very tired. Swimming seemed all at once impossible, his feet felt encased in iron, he was so cold and the river bank seemed so far away. Joe struggled to remove his trainers. It took a tremendous effort but at last he managed to pull them off. He struck out for the river bank. Normally he was a strong swimmer but this was no safe swimming pool. Here a powerful current was trying to pull him back out into the middle of the river and he knew that if it succeeded he'd drown. He summoned up all his energy and desperately swam for the bank. Slowly, very slowly he started to make headway, until at last his feet touched the bottom of the river. He grabbed the root of a scrubby tree and with one final lunge managed to haul himself, aching, from the water.

He heaved himself up through the mud, feeling his sodden clothes squelching beneath his body, and sprawled on the bank, gasping for air, trying to get his breath back. He was shaking uncontrollably from the cold. Must keep moving, he thought. Stay here and I'm going to die from hypothermia. Must keep the blood circulating. Must keep moving.

Joe rolled himself wearily over on to his back, shivered as a dribble of icy water ran down his chest, and stared at the sky. The first stars were out. Joe tried to imagine how far away they were. The distances were so great that his brain could never really take them in. White dwarfs, red giants, huge balls of burning gases, incredibly hot, suns so big you could fit our sun and the earth going round it inside them.

The moon was bright – half full – or was it half empty? What did they say? If you looked at half a glass of water and said that it was half full, then you were an optimist, you always looked on the bright side. There was still plenty left to drink. If you said the glass was half empty, you were a pessimist, because half of your drink had gone already. So, was it an optimistic moon or a pessimistic one? The moon was lying on its back, like him, like a rocking-horse runner. Go to sleep. Rock me. Rock me. Light a fire.

Where did that strange thought come from? No, go to sleep. That's it.

Joe opened his eyes. Suddenly he realized he was freezing cold. He was shivering. What was he doing? Going to sleep. No, he mustn't go to sleep. Something hard was digging into his leg. What was it? He pulled himself up and felt in his pocket – a box of matches. That's it! Light a fire. Get warm. With trembling fingers he pushed the little drawer open. Amazing – he could hardly believe it. The matches were dry despite his time in the water.

But what could he burn? Had the marsh dried out enough from all that rain? There would surely be some dry wood and branches about somewhere. All his possessions, including his burner, were on the barge. Of course, the barge. He must run along the river bank and catch it up. Joe stared into the darkness that obscured the river bank. No way would he be able to follow the river at night. The marsh was hard enough to cross in the daytime, when you could see where you were going. It would be impossible now and, anyway, he wasn't really sure of the direction he should be travelling in.

No, take a stock of himself. There would be a path somewhere. Find a path, follow it. Find something to burn. Find a path, build a fire, warm up, dry out. Don't panic. Gingerly he felt his face. It was sore. His arms, too. How many times had he been bitten? More than he could count.

In the distance an owl hooted. Its cry echoed eerily across the dark landscape.

'I hope,' Joe said to the owl, wherever it was, 'you are a

normal owl. Please don't be a giant man-eating owl. I don't think I could cope.'

Close by he heard another hoot. A second owl returning the first call, no doubt. Then he saw it. In a rush of wings that made Joe jump, the owl flew from a bush by the river into the sky. For a moment its body was silhouetted against the moon. Then it was gone.

As Joe stared up at the blossoming stars, momentarily lost in the vastness of the universe, something long, thin and slippery brushed along his leg.

Hannah limped along the path in the darkness, shivering. Somehow she'd twisted her foot. Her clothes were wet and cold and clung to her body. Her shoes were wet, too. Luckily she'd had the presence of mind to take them off before she'd followed Joe into the water. Her ears were still singing from the buzzing of the mosquito swarm and she could feel several lumps forming on her face where she'd been bitten.

The marsh stretched around her in all directions, pale blue in the moonlight, and ahead, in the distance, she could just make out the dark blur of the mountain, the mountain that haunted her dreams. Somewhere near by she heard the plaintive hoot of an owl.

When the mosquito swarm had hit the barge she – and just about every monkey on board, it seemed – had jumped into the river. It was bedlam. How many monkeys had made it back to the barge? she wondered. Could monkeys swim? Could one-armed monkeys swim? Well, if she and Joe ever got back to the barge, they'd find out. If! She'd have to find Joe first, of course. He might not have been washed up on this bank even. He might even now be on the other side of the river.

After she'd made it to the river bank she'd searched for Joe – but had seen no sign of him. If he were on the other bank, of course, she might well have seen the last of him. Then what would she do? Find someone else? That would be a tall order. Finding Joe had been an amazing piece of luck.

The owl hooted again. Some way away another owl cried in reply. Hannah looked up at the sky. The first stars were out. Weren't they beautiful? Every star, Hannah had heard, was the soul of a dead person. That was why, when you wished upon a star, someone would hear your wish. And if you chose the star of someone who had been particularly kind in his or her life, then the wish would be granted. She wondered if her own father was now a star. She felt suddenly sad and alone.

Hannah followed the path she had found. It was quite wide and led away from the few scrappy trees that lined the river bank out on to the wild flatness of the marsh. Some way ahead she could make out a hill and the path seemed to be winding towards it. She could hear the sound of sheep bleating. This is a long way into the marsh for sheep, she thought. As she approached the dark shape of the hill the cries of the sheep grew louder, but above their bleating Hannah could hear something else. The owls again, their ethereal cries now sharper, louder, more urgent.

Then all at once, with an ear-splitting screech, two huge owls dropped from the sky upon her. She threw up her arms to protect her face. She caught a glimpse of two glowing yellow eyes and a hooked beak and talons bearing down on her, then ducked her head from the swipe of a claw aimed at her face. Wildly she looked around – she must escape, but there was nowhere to run. She curled herself into a ball, feeling the beat of wings as the second owl passed her, screeching all the while.

She felt an agonizing pain in her shoulder as the first owl attacked again and sank its claws into her. There was nothing she could do, she knew. The weight of the owl was on top of her now. She could feel its talons biting into her shoulder. She must get up. Try to fight them. It couldn't end like this. She still had so much to do.

Well, Joe thought, there was nothing for it but to move. Action. The shivering had turned to shaking. He knew he had to get warm, maybe dry his clothes a bit, definitely find the barge again and Hannah and Judy. Joe tried to step forward but his foot seemed caught in something and he stumbled and nearly fell. He looked down and caught his breath. A snake. A snake as thick as his arm was coiling around his leg, its body a dull green colour. He kicked at it wildly. Surely there were no snakes on the marsh. But then, there were no monkeys either, and he'd seen them, talked to them even. His foot wouldn't move. He could feel the snake moving. He could see it twisting itself more firmly around his ankle. But the harder he struggled the tighter the snake gripped him.

Wait a minute. There was something wrong here. He looked more closely at the snake. It wasn't a snake at all. It was snake-like, yes. But it was harder, more like the root of a tree. Of course – it was the tendril of a creeper of some kind. There was a rustling in the undergrowth and he saw another tendril snaking towards him, then another. The now familiar panicky feeling gripped him, clutched his stomach. Still he struggled to pull away as he watched the other tendrils slowly sliding closer.

Joe had to work fast. He sat down. He gripped the creeper entwined around his ankle firmly. It felt really unpleasant, moist and slimy. In fact it felt like he had always imagined snakes to feel, until the time he had actually held a real one and discovered it was smooth and warm. Grasping the rubbery creeper as tightly as he could, he tried to untwist it from around his leg. But it was far stronger than he was, and it was tightening its grip all the time.

Joe's leg was beginning to hurt and there were pins and needles in his foot. The two other tendrils were almost upon him. Was this it, then? The end of his adventure to find his father? Any hope of escape from the creeper began to drain away. He summoned up the energy for one last effort to escape – but then he thought, why bother? If he got this tendril off there were the others. He couldn't run. He began to let go of the creeper. He could hear voices. Could he hear them or was he imagining them? He strained his ears. They were soft voices. He couldn't make out what they were saying, just a kind of low gabble. Soothing, almost. The creeper gripping his leg seemed unimportant somehow. But he had to do something. What was it?

One of the owls was circling Hannah, shrieking excitedly, its wings beating the air in a frenzy. Hannah tried to get up and push the owl away. Suddenly there was a deafening explosion, a crash of sound that rolled across the marsh like thunder. Hannah felt the owl on her shoulder disintegrate in a shower of blood and feathers. The other owl disappeared in a confusion of screeches. Hannah looked wildly round to find herself staring into the barrel of a gun. A gun pointing straight at her – and held by an animal.

The animal was bigger than her and stood on its hind legs. Its fur glowed red in the moonlight. Its eyes were expressionless – glaring at her, as though it hadn't made up its mind whether she was a friend or foe, whether to shoot her or not. It watched her silently for a few moments, then swished its big bushy tail and lowered the gun.

'Renaldo,' it said, its voice soft and silky, 'at your service.'

The pain in Hannah's shoulder became too much to bear. She saw the world and its colours fade to black and white. Then she saw nothing. She fainted.

The crash of the gun jolted Joe from his daydream. He tensed. The other tendrils were now upon him, inching their way around his body. But the explosion, quite close, must also have affected the creeper. For a second or two it had relaxed its grip. As the echoes of the shotgun blast rolled around the moonlit landscape like distant drums, Joe made one last effort to free himself and leapt to his feet, his leg and foot sliding from the creeper's grasp. He staggered backwards, away from the weird plant. It could sense him in some way, Joe realized, for it was again moving towards him. He would have to get away – and fast.

As he plunged into the undergrowth, Joe looked around for signs of a path. Nothing. Well, he thought, he should keep to the river bank. He mustn't get himself lost. He ran as fast as he dared, wincing in pain as his bare feet trod on something sharp, a stray bramble or a piece of flint. He should never have discarded his trainers. He jumped over thistles, brambles and all manner of grasses and spindly plants. At last he came to a clearing and stopped. He must surely have outpaced the creeper. He looked behind him warily. No sign of the insinuating tendrils. Out of breath he sat on a rotting tree stump to rest. He had warmed up a bit, but he still felt wet and uncomfortable. This might be the place to try a fire, he thought, and began searching around for suitable materials.

Nearby an owl hooted a mournful cry.

## CHAPTER 12

# RENALDO

Joe felt wet and miserable and still shaken by his experience with the creeper. He looked around. He was sitting beneath a dead tree that rose above him and the wild moonlit marsh like a black exclamation mark. The tree seemed to be saying to the world: here is Joe, alone and defenceless, come and get him. But Joe didn't care. He was too tired to care, shivering in his cold, wet clothes. The tree was bare except for a few spiky branches and the top of its trunk was knotted like a giant's fist raised in anger at whatever might threaten from the sky above. It cast a black moon shadow across the ground around it, which was clear of any vegetation – here the earth was hard and trampled down. How had it got to be like that? Joe wondered. What creatures might have gathered here beneath this dead tree and for what purposes? Joe couldn't imagine – nor did he want to. But the clearing would do for a fire. And the brushwood here seemed dry, thank goodness.

How far had he come from the river? He could hear the murmuring of the flooded current, but he could no longer see the water. He gazed up at the stars, still burning brightly with the light that had travelled a million billion kilometres through space. Joe pulled himself wearily to his feet and started collecting twigs and branches. Even moving seemed an effort. He wondered about the mosquito attack on the barge. How long ago had that been? Not very long – but it *seemed* so long ago. He touched his face. It still felt sore.

At last the twigs were delicately arranged, larger ones overlapping smaller ones, with a few heavier branches put to one side for when the fire caught. His dad had taught him to build a fire like this. For some odd reason it reminded Joe of the Little Pig's house of sticks. A fragile thing, he thought, so carefully constructed, and yet any moment now it would be destroyed. Not by a wolf's huffing and puffing, but by fire.

Joe bent down and took the matches from his pocket. He lit one and held it next to a feathery twig, watching intently as the tiny flame wound itself around the thin framework, grew bigger, brighter, crackled and began to consume the wood. Dark grey smoke curled around the twigs as the fire took hold. Joe smiled. The smell reminded him of Bonfire Night.

The flames glowed with a dazzling yellow light, now orange, now red, shifting lazily through the spectrum of colour. Now the flames were dancing, an eerie purple, red again, orange, yellow, green, blue, casting flickering shadows around the clearing. Joe pricked up his ears. He fancied he could hear the voices again – the voices he had heard earlier, but much clearer this time.

*Sleep, Joe,* they seemed to be saying. *Sleep. Sleep. Close your eyes. You've had such a busy day.*

74

*Joe!*

It was his father's voice, loud, sharp and clear.

Joe opened his eyes and sat up, looking wildly about. Strange shadows danced around the clearing. No, he'd imagined it. It wasn't his father's voice. There was nobody there. The fire was burning merrily, in fact it would burn itself out soon unless he did something. Joe carefully laid the heavier branches on top of the twigs, watching with satisfaction as the flames curled around them. He lay back down and stared up at the dark shadowy branches of the tree, silhouetted against the luminous sky.

Was it his imagination or could he see a face in the tree? A strange face with two huge, pale eyes that stared down at him. The eyes blinked. Then Joe could see what it was. An owl. The owl screeched and launched itself from the branch towards him.

Hannah could feel the arms around her – big, warm, comforting arms. A scent wafted around her – not pleasant but not unpleasant, either. The jogging motion reminded her of her mother carrying her, long ago. There was a nagging pain in her arm but her mother had soothed her. It'll be all right, her mother had said, in her soft, singing voice. There, there, baby. Don't worry. She had fallen from a swing. The picture of her mother's face as she cuddled Hannah was sharp and crystal clear in her mind. 'Is that you, Mum?' she asked. 'Have you come back?' But the smell, the scent. It wasn't her mother, it was a strange, animal scent. She opened her eyes.

Renaldo looked down at her, his brown eyes anxious. His reddish-brown snout was sleek, his nose shiny wet, his teeth sharp, his breath a mixture of spicy sweetness and sour meat. A rivulet of saliva ran down his chin. If it hadn't been for the concerned look in his eyes, Hannah would have suspected him of planning to eat her. Now she knew how Little Red Riding Hood must have felt when she'd met the wolf. But hadn't Red Riding Hood brought all that happened to her upon herself? There was no way this fox could have made a convincing grandma. Gently he stood Hannah down.

'How do you feel?' he asked.

Hannah looked around.

'OK, thank you.'

They were standing on the side of a hill. A cave, like a black smudge, disappeared into the hillside. Above them blazed the stars and a crescent moon. All around them, fenced in, were sheep, mostly asleep but some restlessly shuffling around. Occasionally one would bleat angrily and paw the ground.

'The sheep are in an ugly mood tonight,' Renaldo said. 'It's those owls. I hate 'em. I've been after them for a while. Lost a couple of sheep to them already.'

'Are you a shepherd, then?'

'I'd have thought that was obvious.'

'It's unusual, though, isn't it? I mean, don't foxes usually hunt sheep?'

Renaldo shrugged. 'Traditionally, of course, the fox is a scavenger. I myself am very partial to lamb, especially curried. It's much easier to keep this flock of sheep for food than to go scavenging about – especially in this place – never knowing where the next meal is coming from.

When I'm hungry I just kill a sheep and eat it. Lamb korma's my favourite.'

'Er, you curry the lamb? You cook it?'

'Of course. What's unusual about that?'

'Nothing, I suppose. Don't you eat anything else?'

'Too dangerous. Most things have been got at. I can keep the sheep clear. You must be tired.'

Hannah nodded. 'And wet. And I've twisted my ankle and my arm hurts. My face, too, where I was bitten.'

'You are in a bad way,' the fox laughed. 'Come with me,' he added gently. 'We'll get you out of those wet clothes and I'll have a look at your arm. There are some blankets in the back cave. You probably just need sleep.'

Hannah followed Renaldo into the dark cave entrance.

'Excuse me for asking,' Renaldo said, 'but what were you doing out on the marsh at night anyway?'

Hannah peeled off her wet top. While the fox inspected her shoulder by the pale moonlight that came in through the cave's entrance, Hannah explained about Joe, Judy and the monkeys. She kept the story brief, mentioning Joe's hunt for his father, but not saying much more. Renaldo made no comment on the story. Her shoulder was bruised but luckily the owl's talons hadn't pierced the skin. Her clothes must have protected her.

All of a sudden Hannah felt very tired. She had wondered whether she could trust the fox — but then decided she had little option. The owls might still be around — and where else could she go? And anyway, it was too late now. Perhaps, if they didn't find Joe, the fox would help her. He seemed friendly — and he was certainly strong enough.

The cave led to a smaller one at the back. It was pitch black and smelled even more strongly of the fox's rich, spicy, animal scent. As her eyes adjusted to the darkness of the cave she saw that Renaldo had fashioned a crude bed in the corner from layers of straw over which he'd laid coarse woollen blankets. She took off the rest of her wet clothes and handed them to the fox. Then, gratefully, Hannah lay down and pulled the blankets tightly around her.

'Don't worry,' Renaldo said from the darkness beside her, 'I'll keep an eye out for your friend. Whatever happens, you'll be OK. And I'll hang your clothes out. It will be hot tomorrow. The sun will soon dry them. Maybe I'll build a fire.'

'A fire?' Hannah said, amazed. 'Aren't you afraid of fire?'

The fox chuckled. 'Of course not.'

'Oh ... Good-night, then,' Hannah said, 'and thank you.' She closed her eyes and was asleep almost at once.

Renaldo watched Hannah for a few moments and then bent over her and pulled the blanket gently around her.

'Sweet dreams,' he whispered.

He crept from the cave room and picked up his shotgun. It was his most treasured find. It had taken him hours to saw off the trigger guard so that his paws could operate it. He held it lovingly to his body and surveyed the skies, willing an owl to come within range. He'd found the gun lying by the body of a man near the mountain. The creeper had taken the body and he'd taken the gun. He

78

reloaded it from his precious supply of cartridges, looked up at the moon and spat.

Joe lay by the fire, enjoying the heat that spread down his side. He felt so comfortable. Above him he could see the owl perched on the branch of the tree. He watched fascinated as it screeched and launched itself into the air, as if in slow motion, and fell towards him. Joe couldn't be bothered to move. It was like watching a video. It was only make-believe, wasn't it?

It was about half a metre from him when, at the last moment, the owl veered away and there was a loud, desperate shrieking noise, just outside his line of vision. Joe did nothing. He just lay there, watching the sparks drift lazily overhead, turning burning golden circles against the silver sky, watching as the owl alighted on the black branch, its big eyes blinking, shining gold reflections from the fire. In the owl's mouth hung the dark, limp body of a rat.

Joe could hear the voices again.

*Sleep*, they said. *Sleep*.

That was easy. He didn't need voices to tell him that. He felt so tired. He closed his eyes, listening to the crackling flames as the fire slowly burnt itself out. Listening to other noises, too. The owl above him. Noises on the ground. Someone or something else there, with him, in the clearing. Something was moving around in the darkness. He could hear scraping, slithering noises. Something touched his foot. Joe didn't move. Why bother? The owl had the rat. The owl and the pussycat went to sea ... The fire would keep the wild creatures of the forest at bay.

Animals were scared of fire. His dad would be along soon. Good-night, Owl. Good-night, Pooh. Good-night, Piglet. Good-night, Joe.

Joe fell asleep.

CHAPTER 13

# MUSHROOMS

Hannah woke up in a panic. Silence. Everywhere was pitch black. She'd been dreaming. What was it? Already the dream was slipping away. She'd been at home in the cottage with her mum and dad. Dad had his white coat on and her mum was tugging at it, trying to pull it off. But the memory of the dream had almost gone. Dissolving like snow on water. She wiped a tear from her eye, sat up in the darkness and shivered. It was bitterly cold.

She pulled the roughly woven woollen blanket more tightly around her. She could hear something. There was someone moving about outside. Her eyes could just about make out the cave opening, lit by the pale moonlight. And there, in hazy silhouette, stood a huge dark shape, filling the entrance. Her mouth went dry and she felt her muscles tense. Whatever it was, it was coming in. She shivered again.

The shape changed. It was someone bending over – releasing a burden.

'Are you awake, Hannah?' a familiar voice asked.

Renaldo, of course. It was the fox.

'Quickly, I need your help. I think this must be Joe.'

Slowly, carefully in the darkness, Hannah went over to the fox, trying not to put too much weight on her still aching foot. The rock beneath her bare feet felt damp and cold. Bright moonlight filtered in from outside and she could see Joe clearly, lying on the ground, his face pale, eyes closed, breathing shallowly, sleeping soundly.

'Joe,' Hannah whispered.

She looked up at Renaldo and saw that his face was grave.

'Is he all right?' she asked.

'He seems to be drugged,' Renaldo said. 'I've not been able to wake him. He was lying next to a fire he'd built. That's how I found him. Lucky I went out looking for him. There was a lot of creeper around. It was after him, I think.'

'The creeper? But you escaped it all right – it didn't get you?'

Renaldo chuckled grimly.

'It doesn't bother me any more,' he said. 'This is peculiar, though. Joe looks like he's been affected by the creeper. There's something in its skin – some sort of drug or poison or something. But I was sure I got to him before the creeper did.'

Hannah reached over and laid her hand on Joe's arm. 'His clothes are still wet,' she remarked.

Renaldo felt them. 'You're right. We'd better take them off and dry them. Go and get a blanket. We must keep him as warm as possible.' Hannah went to fetch it. When she returned the fox had already pulled Joe's jeans off and was staring at his leg.

'Look,' the fox said. There was a huge red weal all around Joe's ankle, winding round up to his knee. 'It's the mark of the creeper all right. You take over here and get his wet things off. I'll be as quick as I can. We may not have much time.'

The fox left, leaving Hannah alone with Joe.

Easy for you to say, Hannah thought, as she struggled with Joe's T-shirt. You're a big strong animal. Trying to pull clothes off someone who's unconscious is not a simple thing. Where had Renaldo gone? Hannah wondered, as she finally managed to pull Joe's T-shirt over his head. Did he have an antidote for the creeper's poison? If he did it would prove invaluable. She'd managed to stay out of the creeper's way until now, but next time she might not be so lucky.

When Renaldo had returned, Hannah had Joe wrapped in a blanket. The fox was holding a mug. He handed it to Hannah.

'Here, you can probably manage this better than me,' he said. 'It's made for hands like yours.'

Hannah took the mug. It was dirty and badly chipped. Obviously Renaldo had found it somewhere. There was a dark liquid in the bottom of it that seemed to glow. Hesitantly Hannah took a sniff. The smell was awful. She gagged at the terrible stench and nearly dropped the mug.

'You OK?' the fox asked, concerned.

Hannah held the mug at arm's length and stared at the fox through watery eyes. 'What is this? It's disgusting.'

The fox took the mug from her and sniffed. 'It doesn't smell all that strongly,' he said.

Hannah pulled a face and Renaldo sighed. 'I'll give it to him, shall I?'

Hannah nodded. Gently, Renaldo lifted Joe's head and awkwardly held the mug to his mouth, tipping it back carefully, allowing a little of the liquid to dribble in.

'This is made from mushrooms,' the fox said. 'Not any old mushrooms, though. I found them some time ago, much nearer the mountain than this. I was in the dead wood and the creeper had me surrounded. There were rats everywhere. I thought I'd had my chickens. But I made a dash for it. I jumped over the rats at a place where the creeper had fewer tendrils and ran through an archway formed by two trees which had fallen against each other. I made it and found myself in a huge clearing completely free of the creeper. It was peculiar – as though the creeper was giving the patch of ground a wide berth. The ground was covered with these pale green mushrooms. Of course, being very clever, I immediately linked the absence of creeper with the presence of the mushrooms.'

Joe sighed in his sleep and his body trembled. Renaldo rested a paw on the boy's forehead until the trembling stopped. Renaldo rubbed the rest of the liquid on Joe's leg. 'That should help.'

'How did you get away?' Hannah asked.

'Are you feeling a bit better now?'

Hannah nodded. 'How did you escape from the clearing, from the creeper? Tell me.'

'I just waited in the clearing until the creeper lost interest in me. After that I collected up as many of these

84

mushrooms as I could carry and high-tailed it out of there. Then I experimented with them.'

'Most mushrooms are poisonous, aren't they?' Hannah asked. 'My mother told me never to eat any mushrooms I found growing wild.'

'Some are deadly poisonous,' Renaldo smiled. 'But not these. I give them to my sheep. The creeper leaves them alone now.'

Renaldo gathered Joe up in his arms and took him into the back cave and laid him on the bed of straw. He piled more blankets on him.

'That's all we can do – keep him warm and hope the poison hasn't taken too firm a hold. I'll dry his clothes out with yours.'

Hannah held Joe's hand. It was cold and clammy.

'He seems to be breathing more easily,' she said.

'I suggest you get back to sleep.' Renaldo said. 'There's nothing more we can do for Joe and you need sleep too.'

Hannah knew he was right. There was just room for her to lie next to Joe on the straw. She pulled some blankets around her.

'Good-night,' she said. 'And thanks again.'

Renaldo chuckled. 'My pleasure.'

He gathered up Hannah's and Joe's clothes and made his way outside. Then he rigged up a rope line and hung the clothes on it. How uncomfortable it must be to wear clothes all the time, he thought. He picked up his shotgun and climbed the steep path that led around the hillside to above his cave. There, he sat on his favourite rock and looked down at the marsh below. From his vantage-point he could see the river clearly, glinting in the moonlight.

And along the river the trees. And in the trees he knew, although he couldn't see them, were the owls. Just fly this way, he whispered. Just fly to me. He grasped the gun. I'm ready for you.

## CHAPTER 14

# CURRY FOR BREAKFAST

Hannah dreamed she stood all alone on the deserted beach, gazing up at the mountain. A dazzling sun was rising above the ocean and it was very quiet. Too quiet. There was no sound at all. Even the waves broke silently on the sand. Her mother was collecting driftwood for a fire. Hannah felt happy, just standing there, waiting, watching the colours of the mountain changing as the sun climbed into the sky. Something brushed her leg. She looked down and screamed. It was the creeper. It was all around her. She turned to run but tripped. The creeper was upon her, covering her. She could feel it on her face, pressing her against the ground, suffocating her. Wet tentacles slid over her face, trying to find a way in, through her mouth, through her nose . . . Hannah struggled to open her eyes.

*Hi ho! Good-morning. Hello. Good-morning. Wake up. Wake up. Come on. It's me.*

Hannah was staring at Judy's face. She was breathing dog breath all over her. Hannah pulled herself up.

'Yeuch!' she said, then she threw her arms around Judy,

laughing. 'You gave me a fright. I was having a nightmare.'

The dog was wagging her tail furiously. Renaldo was standing in the cave entrance, silhouetted against the warm golden light seeping into the cave.

'A friend of yours?' he chuckled.

Hannah remembered Joe. Where was he? She looked frantically around as memories of the previous evening came back to her.

*See yah. I can smell food.*

Hannah watched as the dog bounded out. She rubbed the sleepy bits from the corners of her eyes.

'What's the time?'

Renaldo shrugged.

'Mid-morning. We don't have clocks and watches here, all that stuff. Catch.'

He tossed Hannah her clothes. They felt warm and dry. She sniffed them – clean, too. Surely Renaldo hadn't washed them for her? But no – there were still smears of dried mud on them.

'Is Joe OK?' she asked.

'He's fine. The mushroom mixture must have done the trick. How are you feeling?'

'I ache.'

Gingerly Hannah felt her arm. It hurt. Even in the dim light of the cave she could see the purple bruises that had formed. She looked at her ankle. It didn't appear to be swollen. She'd been lucky. She stood up and tested it with her weight. It ached a bit but was otherwise OK. Her face itched, too. But the mosquito bites didn't feel too bad. How else did she feel? Relieved that Joe had recovered – although thinking about Joe gave her a pang of guilt when

88

she thought of what she was doing. She felt pleased that Judy had found them. And she felt hungry.

'I don't suppose there's any chance of some breakfast?' she asked.

'Of course. Get dressed and join us. It's a beautiful day.'

Hannah blinked in the bright sunlight. The sky was swimming-pool blue. She was outside Renaldo's cave, looking down on the marsh. She stood for a few moments, breathing in the fresh air and staring into the distance, thinking. Somewhere out there was civilization, somewhere beneath the dark grey clouds that hung heavy over the horizon. Somewhere out there was her new home. Her foster-parents were friendly enough, but she wanted her mother back. Somehow she had to get Joe to the cottage on the mountain. It was her only hope.

From here Hannah could clearly see the line of trees that marked the river where the mosquitoes had attacked the day before. Below she could see Renaldo's sheep in their pen and nearby she could hear voices. And she could smell meat cooking. She put her thoughts to one side and followed the sounds and smells coming from around the side of the hill. There, in a natural alcove surrounded on three sides by rocky walls, sat Joe, Renaldo and Streak. A small fire blazed merrily in front of them, sending a thin plume of woody smoke into the blue above.

'Joe!' she cried with relief. 'You're all right.'

'As you can see,' Joe said, smiling. 'You look a mess.' He was holding a stick with a piece of meat skewered on the end above the glowing embers of the fire.

'And Streak,' Hannah said. 'What are you doing here? Where are the others? Where's the crew?'

'Ho, me hearties,' Streak whooped. 'We're waiting for you two. Most of us made it back to the barge after the attack – including your dog. She was heavy to pull aboard, I can tell you. Why they don't make dogs with arms I'll never know.'

'Where *is* Judy?'

'Chasing a stick I expect,' said Joe, 'or something equally interesting.'

'I found an old sheep's bone for her,' Renaldo said. 'She's around somewhere.'

'So,' Streak continued, 'we discussed what to do. Most of the older monkeys weren't interested in going on. All they want is a peaceful life, after all they've been through. But I thought – no. Joe needs help to find his dad – and we *are* pirates after all, and pirates *help* people. So . . .'

'Er . . . not help, exactly, not pirates,' Joe said.

'Is there any food left?' Hannah asked. 'I'm starving.'

'Of course,' Renaldo said. 'Come on round the fire, there's plenty of room.' He took a sharpened stick from a pile and handed it to Hannah.

'There's some meat soaking in the pot. Stab a bit, then cook it. It's a curry. Delicious. Lamb korma in your honour.'

Hannah took the stick and peered into the pot. The pieces of lamb were marinating in something, but it certainly wasn't curry. The cooking meat did smell delicious though – so whatever it was, she was game to try it. She poked about with her stick, ignoring the bits of liver and other rather unsavoury parts of the animal that she didn't wish to know about, until she found a normal piece of meat and, after a couple of unsuccessful attempts, managed to spear it.

Hannah squeezed into the circle and began to roast the piece of meat over the flame. She stole a glance at Joe. So Streak was going to help. But was that enough? Yesterday Joe had said that he was definitely turning back.

'Enjoying the korma?' Renaldo asked. 'Great, isn't it? I love curry.'

Hannah didn't like to tell him that this definitely wasn't curry. And it certainly wasn't korma.

Joe gave Renaldo a sidelong glance but he said nothing, either.

'I'm glad we can't see the sheep from here,' Joe said. 'I don't think I'd want to be eating lamb and looking at the sheep at the same time.'

'Traditionally, of course,' Renaldo said, 'foxes have never really been worried about that sort of thing. Most foxes, I believe, eat their meat raw. Rather barbaric.' The fox stopped chewing for a moment, as though lost in thought. 'I sometimes think that I'm not like other foxes.'

'You can say that again,' Joe said.

'I sometimes think,' Renaldo said, 'that I'm not like other foxes.'

Joe laughed but stopped when he saw the fox looking at him oddly. They all continued to eat in silence.

Hannah kept an eye on Joe. He seemed to be enjoying himself – apart from Renaldo's odd reaction to his laughter. Perhaps he would go on, if he was having a good time. She would have to wait and see, bide her time. She wondered whether the fox did have a sense of humour or was he really puzzled by Joe's laughter? They said that animals couldn't laugh. But then, that was in a world where animals didn't talk. Not here on the marsh.

They continued to eat in silence, breathing in the crisp morning air, the wood smoke and the strange mixture of animal scents. Hannah was only on her third piece of meat when Streak suddenly jumped up.

'Time to go, me hearties. Time to get shipshape and Bristol fashion.'

What does that mean? Hannah wondered. She suspected that the monkey didn't know either.

Streak stretched. 'Come on. The others won't wait all day. Must be quick, no landlubbing or they'll be gone.'

Joe stood up. 'I'd wash your face if I were you,' he said to Hannah.

'What?'

Renaldo chuckled. 'There's a bucket of water over there.'

Hannah went to the bucket and splashed water over her face. She rubbed her hands through her hair. Bits of feather drifted through the air. Of course, the owl that Renaldo had shot. She was still covered in dried blood and feathers. She washed them off as best she could.

'Is that better?' she asked.

'Fine,' Joe said.

It certainly felt better, she thought. Hannah eyed the food. She was still hungry, but she didn't want to risk missing the barge. Streak was probably right about the monkey crew. She doubted if they could be relied upon to wait. And Joe seemed anxious to resume the journey. She didn't want to do anything that might risk him changing his mind. She would just have to be hungry. She could bear it a bit longer. It would all be over soon, anyway. Once they got to the cottage.

They stood at the top of the path and thanked Renaldo. Judy bounded ahead, an ungainly bone in her mouth.

'Ah,' Renaldo said, suddenly remembering something. 'Wait a moment.'

He turned and disappeared into the cave. He came out holding a Coke bottle and handed it to Joe.

'It's creeper repellent,' Renaldo told him. 'It's what we gave you yesterday when you were unconscious. The creeper is covered with a slimy substance that contains a drug or a poison or something. That's the antidote.'

Joe took it. He wasn't sure what the creeper was — the last thing he remembered before waking up in the cave was jumping into the water when the mosquitoes attacked. But the repellent sounded like it would come in useful.

'Thanks,' he said and stuffed the bottle in his pocket.

'Hurry along. No time to dawdle,' Streak said.

They hurried down the hill towards the trees and the river.

Hannah glanced back, to see Renaldo standing on top of the hill. He had his back to them and was staring in the opposite direction. I know what he's staring at, she thought, the mountain, where all paths lead, and she shuddered. She wished she didn't have to go back.

They had nearly reached the river when Joe called a halt.

'What was that?' he asked.

They all listened.

They had reached the shelter of the trees. There was a

loud splash, the sound of something heavy being dropped in the water, followed by a long, low groaning noise.

'Oh dear,' Streak said, and ran ahead.

They followed. The path led around a corner and there was the barge, tied up among some bulrushes.

From the other side of the barge came the loud splashing noise and again the long, low groan.

Judy was behind them now, hanging back, obviously uncertain of what might be happening on the barge. Cautiously Hannah and Joe made their way up the gangplank.

CHAPTER 15

# TOAD IN THE HOLD

The deck was on a slope and they felt the barge shift uneasily beneath them as they walked cautiously across the worn boards towards the groaning noise. All the monkeys were lined up on the opposite side of the barge where four of them were struggling with a body, one of the older, grey-haired monkeys. They were lifting it on to the rail. Joe and the others came to a halt and watched the strange scene. At last the monkeys had the body perched on the rail, then with a final push the dead monkey toppled into the water. There was a soft splash and another eerie groan went up from the onlookers.

Unnoticed, Joe, Hannah, Judy and Streak joined them. Joe peered at the river moving sluggishly by, shielding his eyes against the dazzling arrows of light reflected on the water's surface. He could see several bodies, dark against the brightness, like dustbin bags, floating lazily away from the barge. It was obviously a burial service, like one for sailors who die at sea. Joe glanced round at all the solemn faces staring at the water. Suddenly he realized that there were no one-armed monkeys. He looked back at the

95

water. Had all the one-armed monkeys died, then? What had they died of – and why them? And why all of them? Perhaps Streak would have the answer.

Then, as he watched, the still surface of the water began to shimmer and ripples appeared. The surface became more agitated, now it was churning, specks of foam mixed in with the writhing water. The bodies were rocking to and fro and the river looked as though it were boiling. A fish dived into the air and at once disappeared into the boiling spume. One by one the bodies disappeared, pulled under by whatever fish were causing the waters to churn. Were they piranha fish? wondered Joe. Then, as suddenly as it had begun, the waters began to quieten and within a couple of minutes the river was back to normal. Only the dark red stain of blood gave any clue that something horrible had happened.

A terrible silence hung over the barge and then the monkeys turned, as one – as if responding to an unspoken cue – and drifted back to their various duties on the barge.

'What was that all about?' Joe whispered to Hannah.

Hannah shrugged and grimaced. Streak was looking unbearably sad. Even Judy seemed to have caught the mood. Her tail was held between her legs. Her big brown eyes looked up at Joe and she gave a little whimper.

'There, there,' Joe said soothingly and stroked her head. 'It's OK, don't worry.'

Joe heard the scraping noise of the gangplank being pulled on board and was at once aware of the birds singing in the trees and the buzz of insects from the river bank. He felt the barge move as it pulled slowly away from the shore towards the middle of the river.

Suddenly he had a strong feeling, a feeling that he recognized. Once he had been in a car and the driver was going much too fast, but there was nothing he could do about it. The feeling was scary and exciting – but he knew he would rather have been somewhere else.

Joe had to admit that part of him was enjoying all this. It was an adventure. It was weird, though, this strange world where animals talked, but he knew, despite his curiosity, that he wanted to go home. He hated having no control over what was happening. He felt as if the barge was taking him somewhere – somewhere that he felt sure he didn't want to go. He had an uneasy feeling that the boat was being drawn downstream by some dark force towards something nasty, something evil. Joe didn't relish the thought of travelling back across the marsh. Who knew what other horrors they'd meet? The best thing would be to turn the barge around and go back up the river.

Joe found his rucksack where he'd left it. He put the bottle Renaldo had given him into the bag. He kept trying to remember what had happened after the mosquito attack the night before, but the memory was elusive, as though what had happened had been a dream that he couldn't recall, however hard he tried.

Joe looked around. Hannah was staring pensively at the water and Judy was nowhere to be seen. The barge was eerily quiet. Streak was perched on the rail at the bow, staring ahead. The old barge was now in the middle of the river, in the grip of the current, and being taken steadily downstream. Joe walked over to Streak.

'Are you all right?' he asked.

Streak glanced at him, then stared back at the river, not speaking.

Joe looked at his odd friend.

'Why did all those monkeys die?'

Slowly Streak turned to Joe and his small hand alighted on Joe's arm.

'They were twins,' the monkey murmured.

Joe thought about that for a moment. He recalled his conversation with Hannah.

'Do you mean they were all born at the same time?' he asked.

Streak nodded. 'Yes. They were all born together and they died together. We were the younger generation – we were born at the same time, too. All of us in the cages. They were the elders and they set us free. That's why we're so sad. Then we all escaped. But I was somehow different. I don't know why. I led them away. We've been wandering a long time.'

Streak scratched himself.

'All of the time dodging the rats. Then we found this barge. At last we thought we were safe. And we were sailing away from our cages, too. But now we seem to be heading back.'

Joe nodded. 'You know you said you'd help me find my father?'

'Yes,' the monkey said.

'I don't think he's here. I want to go home. Let's just turn this thing around and go back.'

Streak looked up. 'I'm not really sure how to do that. I'm not really a sailor, you know.'

Joe laughed. 'I know,' he said kindly.

A thought occurred to Joe. 'Do you know where this river goes?' he asked Streak.

'Back to the cages.'

'No,' Joe said, 'I don't mean that. The river flows out to the sea.'

'The sea?'

Joe nodded.

'What's the sea?'

'It's a vast expanse of water. That's where we're heading. And across the sea is your home.'

Streak was looking perplexed. 'Our cages? They're across the sea?'

'No,' Joe said. 'Across the sea is your home. Your real home. Africa.'

Joe doubted if the barge could really sail to Africa. But he did know that once they reached the sea they would all be safe. They'd all be away from the marsh. It was a much better bet, he now realized, than going back the way they'd come.

'Africa,' Streak said, as though trying the word out. 'It has a nice sound to it.'

'Even if you can't reach Africa,' Joe said, 'you'll be safe. You'll be far away from this place.'

A cry rang through the still air. 'Boat ahoy!'

Streak was immediately alert. He perched on the rail, scanned the river ahead, and pointed.

'I see her. Propel to repair boarders,' he shrieked.

The mood of despondency that had settled on the boat was at once forgotten as monkeys began running around excitedly. Hannah rushed over to Joe and Judy began barking.

'What is it?' Hannah asked.

'Look,' Joe said. 'Another boat.'

It was a large cabin cruiser, but smaller than the barge. It was some way out from the shore. Joe wondered why it wasn't drifting with the current, then he noticed the half-submerged tree trunk against its hull. It was stuck. The boat looked deserted and bedraggled – it was badly in need of a coat of paint.

The monkey crew manoeuvred the barge alongside the boat and threw the anchor overboard.

'Come on,' Streak urged. 'Last one on's a dumb parrot!'

Joe looked at Hannah and raised his eyebrows. She smiled. Streak's command of English was extraordinary.

The gangway was hauled along the deck and hoisted across the gap between the boats.

'What do you think?' Joe asked Hannah. 'It looks sinister.'

'What do you mean?'

'You know – wiggy, scary.'

'Don't be silly,' Hannah said. 'It's just a boat.'

Streak, followed by two of the crew, scuttled across the plank. Joe balanced himself on the rail, helped by Hannah.

'It's a bit precarious,' he said.

Streak and the others were already at the cruiser's cabin door. As Joe concentrated on crossing the plank, he heard the monkeys going into the cabin. He was half-way across, poised high above the dark waters of the river, when the monkeys reappeared, waving their arms in agitation.

'Hurry, me hearty,' Streak yelled.

For a moment Joe lost his concentration, and nearly lost his balance. He steadied himself and took two quick steps across the plank and jumped on to the deck of the other boat. Streak and the others were standing uncertainly by the door of the cabin. Joe turned and helped Hannah on board. Judy followed. She was snarling and wagging her tail at the same time.

*What is it? What is it? Let me see. A rabbit, is it? I'll see it off, see if I don't. Oh, yes.*

But Joe noticed that Judy was hanging back. No doubt she remembered her earlier encounter with a rabbit. The children approached the cabin with caution. The door had swung shut. Joe tensed. He'd seen some scary things in the last couple of days and, not for the first time, he wished he was somewhere else. Tentatively he pushed the door open and peered in. There was a loud hissing sound and he stepped back in alarm. Then, with Hannah close behind him and the monkeys in tow, he took half a step into the gloom of the cabin. He could hear the hissing sound coming from the darkness inside.

As his eyes adjusted to the gloom he could see that the cabin was bare. Cobwebs hung from the corners and he could smell the scent of decay. The only light came from the door and two portholes, covered in dust and grime.

Then he saw it. It was directly opposite them, sitting by a hatch which led to steps down into the hull of the boat. It hissed again, but for some reason Joe felt like he wanted to laugh. For there, on the floor, sat a large brown toad.

'It's a frog,' Hannah said in amazement.

Joe corrected her. 'No, it's a toad. Look at its skin, it's dry and knobbly.'

'It's big, isn't it?'

Joe smiled. 'Well, it would be, wouldn't it? Everything

on the marsh is larger than life.' He peered at the animal. 'It looks a bit like a Fowler's toad. See that bright yellow stripe down its back?'

The toad hissed again and moved back slowly into the darkness at the top of the steps. It stopped, its eyes glinting in the gloom, staring straight at Joe.

A terrible smell wafted across the cabin.

'Ugh,' Hannah said, screwing up her face.

'It's warning us,' Joe said. 'Be careful – toads can be poisonous.'

Toads weren't usually really dangerous to people, Joe knew, although some could give you a bit of a rash, but out here on the marsh where the laws of nature seemed to have been turned upside-down, this one might be lethal.

The toad gave a little cry, turned and disappeared down the hatch.

They stood in silence, wondering what to do next. Judy growled. Then the toad reappeared. It made the same small cry and again turned and disappeared.

'I think it wants you to follow it,' Hannah said.

'Yes,' Streak said excitedly. 'Go on, shipmate. It wants you to follow it.'

Joe protested. 'Me? It wants us *all* to follow it.'

He looked at the others. No one seemed prepared to move.

Judy growled again and before anyone could stop her she rushed towards the hatch.

'Oh no,' Joe said.

Judy disappeared. When she came back, she was making whimpering noises. Hannah bent down and stroked her.

'What is it?' she asked. 'What did you see?'

'It can't be too bad,' Joe said. 'Look at her tail.'

Judy's tail was wagging wildly.

*Come on. Come on. It's all right.*

Joe shrugged. 'I suppose it's OK,' he said. 'Don't worry. I'll go first.' And he led the way down into the dank, damp darkness.

## CHAPTER 16

# TREE

The hatch was quite wide. Joe's hand touched the wall to his right for guidance in the dark, his foot feeling for the next step down. He could hear the others around him as they descended cautiously. Something brushed his face, making him jump. It's OK, he told himself, just a cobweb. He could feel the dampness of the wall. His fingers touched something damp and clammy – fungus, he guessed. He moved his hand quickly away. The smell grew stronger, rising from the darkness below to meet them.

'It smells like rotting meat,' Hannah whispered in Joe's ear.

It was an unhealthy smell, that was certain. Joe felt the now familiar gnawing sensation in the pit of his stomach. At the bottom they stood in the darkness, letting their eyes adjust to the blackness and their noses become accustomed to the smell.

'What a stench,' Joe whispered. 'Can you see anything?'

'No,' Hannah said. 'Wait – I've an idea.'

Joe waited nervously. He could hear the monkeys close by, breathing and making tiny twittering noises. He could hear Judy panting. Suddenly there was a loud scraping sound followed by light. Hannah had found a shutter to a porthole. She released another. Now they could see they were in a small room.

In its centre was an upturned table and a couple of chairs, all covered in dust and cobwebbed from neglect. There was a sharp intake of breath as they all saw it at the same time. There, in the gloomy light of the cabin, was the body of a pig – a huge, fat, bloated pig. And on the rump of the pig sat the toad, tears falling from its eyes.

They all stood and stared.

'Look at that,' Joe said, and pointed. The pig's skin was covered with red weals. 'It looks like it's been whipped.'

'No, I don't think it's that,' Hannah said, studying the marks. 'I think the creeper must have got it.'

At the mention of the creeper the monkeys started shuffling their feet anxiously.

'Renaldo mentioned something about a creeper,' Joe said.

Hannah looked at Joe, puzzled. 'When Renaldo brought you back to the cave you were unconscious,' Hannah said. 'The creeper must have attacked you. Don't you remember?'

Joe shook his head.

'You had similar marks on your leg. Surely you must remember that?'

'No,' Joe said. 'I thought I'd just fallen asleep.'

'You must have somehow blanked the memory out,' Hannah said.

The toad gave another forlorn hiss.

Now Streak and the other monkeys were pacing about anxiously.

'Time to go, me hearties,' Streak said, tugging at Joe's arm. 'Don't want the creeper to catch us, do we?'

Joe looked around. 'There's no creeper here,' he said.

'It'll be back, make no bones about it,' Streak said. 'Let's go.'

'But what about the pig and the toad?' Joe asked.

'We'll leave the pig here,' Hannah said. 'It's dead and there's not much point trying to move it. It will be contaminated. The creeper gives out some kind of poison. That's what knocked you out.'

Joe shivered. Hannah walked carefully up to the toad. 'Do you want to come with us?' she asked it softly.

The toad blinked.

Streak was becoming very agitated now. 'Let's go, me hearties, let's go.'

The cruiser moved in the current. Judy gave a little bark and scrambled up the steps.

'Come on,' Streak said, and he and the other monkeys quickly followed the dog.

Joe joined Hannah.

'Do you want to come with us?' he asked the toad.

Another tear formed in its eye but still it didn't move.

'Was the pig your friend?' Hannah asked.

The toad remained motionless, blinking, as another tear dribbled down its knobbly skin.

'Come on,' Joe said. 'We'd better go.'

'I suppose so,' Hannah replied.

Joe and Hannah found their way back to the deck of

the cruiser. The sunlight made them blink. At once the air was full of bird-song and Joe breathed in the fresh, clean scents of the river. He hadn't realized just how damp and smelly it had been below deck.

Judy and the monkeys were already on the barge, waiting anxiously for Joe and Hannah. They negotiated the plank carefully and were soon returned to the safety of the barge. The crew were about to pull the gangplank back when Hannah stopped them.

'Look,' she said.

The toad had appeared from the cabin, blinking furiously in the daylight.

'Come on, then,' Hannah called to it.

It hopped slowly across the deck, over the gangplank and on to the barge.

Hannah reached down and carefully picked it up.

'Welcome aboard,' she said, smiling.

The toad gave a little croak and started struggling in her hands.

'I don't think it likes being picked up,' Joe said.

Carefully Hannah put it down on the deck.

'Anchors awash!' Streak yelled. The gangplank was retrieved, the anchor was pulled up and the barge slowly drifted back to the middle of the river to continue its journey to the sea.

The sun was low in the sky as Joe lay on the roof of the cabin. He was watching a fluffy white cloud, tinged with pink, drift by high overhead. The cloud looked like a huge eagle, but as he watched the shape changed to that of a human face. He'd taken off his T-shirt and the slight breeze rippled against his bare skin. It felt good after the heat of the day. He'd almost forgotten why he was here. The quest to find his dad seemed to belong to another time, another place. He felt relaxed and drowsy – as though he could lie here on the boat, drifting effortlessly downstream, for ever. Swifts and swallows darted above the barge, catching their evening meal.

As Joe thought about his past life, his home, his friends from school, he became aware of a commotion on the deck below.

'Joe!' He heard his name being called, but it hardly registered.

'Joe!' There it was again.

Reluctantly he sat up and peered down. Hannah was waving at him. I wonder what she wants, he thought. He gathered his T-shirt and slipped it on. He climbed down the brass-runged ladder to the deck, rubbing the sleep from his eyes. Had he been asleep, then? He must have been. His face felt sore. Too long in the sun. Since it was October he'd not thought to pack any sun cream.

The barge was still in the middle of the river but the anchor had been dropped. Streak and the monkeys, and Judy and the toad, were gathered around Hannah at the bow of the barge. Joe joined them.

'What's happening?' he asked.

'Look,' Hannah said, pointing ahead.

Joe gasped. There in the distance was a mountain. But that *was* impossible. Talking animals? Well, that seemed quite reasonable now. But a mountain? There was no mountain on the marsh. How had it got there? Then he remembered that Hannah had mentioned a mountain. So had Streak.

'It's amazing,' Joe said.

Hannah gave him a questioning look. 'What?'

'How did it get there?' Joe asked.

Hannah shrugged. 'The storm, I expect. There was quite a wind.'

Now it was Joe's turn to look questioningly.

'The storm?' Joe said incredulously. 'The storm *blew* the mountain there?'

'No, not the mountain,' Hannah said impatiently. 'Look – in the river.'

Joe adjusted his gaze. Now he could see what they were all excited about. Here the river banks were heavily wooded and a huge tree had blown down. Its great trunk stretched from one bank to the other, forming a bridge – and a barrier. Bits of weed and driftwood clung to its branches. There was no way the barge could pass.

'What now, shipmates?' Streak piped up.

Joe suddenly felt despondent. He'd given up the quest for his father and that had lifted a weight from his mind. Now he was simply enjoying the journey, knowing that they would soon reach the sea and they would all be free of this terrible place. But the fallen tree could change all that. He had no desire to set foot on the marsh again. The marsh, he was convinced, was evil.

'Well,' he said, 'I suppose we'll have to move it.'

'Whatever we do,' Hannah said, 'it will have to wait till the morning.'

Joe looked up. The setting sun hung low over the

horizon like a fiery red ball and the sky was alive with the songs of birds, singing out the last few minutes of daylight.

Joe looked back at the tree. 'I'm not sure how we'll move it though. It's enormous. Whatever happens, I don't want to go on to the marsh again.'

'What do you mean?' Hannah asked, surprised.

'What I said. We're sailing to the sea. Then I'm going home.'

'But what about your dad?' she said, a note of panic in her voice.

'I already told you that,' Joe said impatiently. 'I don't believe he's here.' Joe turned to Streak. 'I don't suppose we have any cutting gear on board, do we? Saws, axes, anything like that?'

'I'll check it out,' Streak said.

'We'll move it somehow,' said Joe. But, as he looked at the huge, darkening shape that blocked their way, he didn't feel very confident that they could shift it. Well, maybe if they applied some science to the problem. He tried to remember what he'd learned about ropes and pulleys. There must be a way to shift it. But it was too dark now. Hannah was right, it would have to wait until the morning.

## CHAPTER 17

# THE DEAD WOOD

Joe and Hannah lay on top of the cabin, Joe's favourite spot on the barge. He was in his sleeping-bag and Hannah was covered by a scruffy blanket that she'd found below deck. Judy was sleeping at the foot of the ladder. Occasionally her snuffly sleep noises drifted up to them, blending with the gentle lapping of the river and the sounds of the night.

Joe and Hannah were both gazing up at the night sky, lit by millions of stars, like the silver breath of jewels on a black window-pane.

'You knew the mountain was there, didn't you?' Joe said.

'Yes,' Hannah replied. 'Actually, it's not really a mountain. Just a huge hill. It's pretty impressive though, isn't it?'

'It is,' Joe said. 'It's incredible that the marsh has suddenly produced a mountain. I mean, I know for a fact there is no mountain on the marsh. But what I really don't understand is this. How did you know the mountain was there? I can only think of one explanation. You've been here before.'

Hannah was silent for a moment before replying. 'Yes, you're right,' she said. 'I was here . . . er . . . quite recently. And, I know I should have told you this before, but I saw your dad.'

'What?' Joe yelled, sitting bolt upright. 'What do you mean you saw him? Where? On the mountain?'

'Yes. On the mountain.'

Joe stared at Hannah. He couldn't believe what he was hearing.

'Then why didn't you tell me before?'

'I didn't want to frighten you.'

Hannah had seen his father on the mountain and she hadn't wanted to frighten him? What on earth did she mean?

'What's going on?' Joe asked her angrily.

'We've got to go there and rescue him.'

Joe looked at Hannah, still staring up at the night sky. But she was avoiding his gaze. Something didn't ring true. He wasn't sure he believed her.

'What does my father look like?'

'He's tall.'

'How tall? Six foot?'

She nodded.

'And is he dark? Black hair?'

'Yes,' Hannah said eagerly. 'And he's trapped on the mountain. The creeper has him.'

'You're lying.'

'I'm not,' Hannah said. 'It's true.'

'He's not six foot,' Joe said. 'He's quite short – and he's blond.'

'Well, I only saw him from a distance.'

'You're lying,' Joe said. 'You were there – but you didn't see him, did you?'

Hannah started to cry. Joe lay back down and tried to relax a little. He felt wound up.

'I need your help,' Hannah said through her sobs. Joe ignored her, thinking back to the time they'd met. She had been determined to come along. She knew the mountain was there and she'd planned to visit it all along. And, he suddenly realized, she wanted *him* to go there with her. It had been her idea to go through the fence. And he'd gone along with it. Now she'd lied about his father. Joe stared up at the stars spinning through space as all kinds of thoughts spun through his mind.

'Why were you there? What's on the mountain?' he asked Hannah at last.

'It never was a firing-range. It's a scientific base,' Hannah said. 'They were doing secret experiments on animals.'

That thought had crossed Joe's mind before. It would explain the monkeys and the cages that Streak had talked about.

'It's called genetic engineering,' Hannah said, 'but I don't really understand it.'

Joe remembered how it had once been explained to him by a teacher. 'Think of a seed,' his teacher had said. 'It's a tiny thing but it grows into a complicated organism like, say, a sunflower. That's a huge thing – all from a tiny seed. All the information a flower needs to grow is contained in that tiny seed. It's stored in code, like the information stored on a computer disk, but so small you'd need a powerful microscope to see it. That seed grows into a complicated flower and – and this is important – it *always* grows into a sunflower. But scientists can change the information that's in the seed. They can alter it so that the seed grows into a different-colour sunflower – or a bigger sunflower – or one that's resistant to diseases.' Joe had been fascinated. But on the mountain they were doing it to animals.

'They were breeding animals?' Joe asked incredulously. 'They were changing them? Doing experiments on them?'

'Yes,' Hannah said. 'But it all went horribly wrong. They were trying to make animals intelligent. And plants, too. That's how the creeper grew. The whole marsh is contaminated.'

'You were trying to get me to go there with you, weren't you?'

'Yes,' Hannah said softly. 'I should have told you all about it. I'm sorry. But I have to go back to my house. That's where it is, on the mountain. That's how I know all about it. Will you help me? It's important.'

'No,' Joe said. 'I won't.'

'Please let me explain.'

'No. I've had enough of your lies.'

He turned away from her, pulling his sleeping-bag tightly around him, staring angrily at the dark shapes of the trees along the river bank. She'd taken him for a fool. 'If you think I'm going anywhere near the place, you're mad,' he said harshly.

'Please?'

'No, and that's final.' There was no way he was going to the mountain. In the morning they would somehow move the tree and then he was getting out of here.

Joe lay listening to the sounds of the night. He thought of all the weird things he'd seen on the marsh. Scientists had done all that. They'd experimented with things that they had no business experimenting with and now the whole marsh was suffering. He thought about the monkeys and about Renaldo, and Judy, too. What had Hannah said? The whole marsh was contaminated? It was wicked. As soon as he got home he'd report it. He'd tell the newspapers. He'd go on television. He would tell the whole world about the horrors of the marsh.

Joe felt incredibly tired. The things he'd seen during the last few days tumbled through his mind. The strange plants, the weird insect life, the rats. The barge swayed gently beneath him. Somewhere the toad croaked mournfully. An owl hooted. And at last Joe fell fretfully asleep.

When he woke up the sun was climbing in the sky – and Hannah was nowhere to be seen.

It was another glorious morning. The sky was clear and a warm breeze blew along the river, rippling the surface of the water. A huge dragon-fly whirred by, its wings a flash of gleaming turquoise. Joe washed himself in a bucket of cold water and had a pee over the side, when he hoped no one was looking. Not that any of the boat's other inhabitants worried where they emptied their bladders. This was why he and Hannah slept above deck. The stench down below was unbearable.

Joe still couldn't get over the fact that Hannah had lied to him. That she had been trying to lure him to the mountain. Now she said she needed his help. Why hadn't she asked him in the first place? Well, if she'd gone to the mountain on her own, that was fine by him.

Joe cooked himself some fish for breakfast. He was already sick of the taste and smell of boiled fish. If only he had a frying pan and some fat. Then he could fry it. He swore he'd never eat boiled fish again. What he wouldn't give for a big, fat, juicy hamburger.

Joe had organized a search for Hannah – but it was no use. She had gone. She was nowhere on the barge. She must have crept away in the middle of the night, although he couldn't think how she had crossed the water. Maybe she swam. He wouldn't have fancied his chances – not after seeing what those bloodthirsty fish did to the bodies of the dead monkeys the day before. So, she had gone to the mountain, although why she wanted to go there he couldn't imagine. Well, good riddance, he thought.

Joe walked around the side of the barge to help the monkeys. They had manoeuvred the boat closer to the massive tree trunk blocking the river and, Joe noticed, they'd found some ropes. Streak was busy trying to organize his crew to pull the tree to one side, to allow the barge to pass. Joe felt sorry for them. He couldn't bear to think what their life must have been like before they escaped.

He watched them for a bit, trying to figure out if there wasn't a better way to move the tree. But all the time his thoughts kept returning to Hannah. She needed his help, she'd said. Why hadn't he asked her more? He was angry, that's why. He hadn't been thinking straight. Maybe he should go after her. But why? To help, of course. No, he wasn't going to risk his life chasing after her. She should have told him the truth from the beginning.

He looked up at the mountain, black and menacing, silhouetted against the clear blue sky, then went to join his friends. The monkeys had secured the gangplank to the side of the tree. Streak, wielding an axe that was obviously too heavy for him, was rushing around giving orders to his bemused crew, who in turn rushed around and got in one another's way. A friendly fight would then break out and Streak would screech for quiet. When calm was finally restored he would give more orders and the process would begin all over again. Joe watched for a few minutes, grinning. It was time to help them.

He was still thinking about Hannah. The monkeys were terrified of the creeper and he remembered what Hannah had said. It had attacked him on the shore. But he had got away. Surely it couldn't be too bad. He couldn't just sail away and leave her, could he? Whatever it was that had made her leave the barge to go back to the mountain must have been important. He made up his mind. Against his better judgement he would go after her. If he hurried he might catch her up and find out what this was all about. Perhaps he could persuade her to come back to the barge.

Hurriedly, before he changed his mind, he packed his bits and pieces into his rucksack. He called Judy. She would be able to follow Hannah's scent, he felt sure. Then he told Streak what he planned to do.

Streak became very agitated. 'But we're going to Africa,' Streak said. 'To the sea.'

'I won't be long,' Joe said. 'I can't let Hannah go there on her own, can I?'

'But what about the creeper?' Streak asked.

'Don't worry,' Joe said bravely, more bravely than he felt. 'I'll keep out of the creeper's way. You just move that tree, then wait for me. I'll be back soon, you'll see.'

Well, he thought, having made up his mind to go on this suicide mission, there seemed to be no reason to hang about any longer. And so he took a deep breath and climbed on to the gangplank. The monkeys fell silent and moved aside to let him pass. Once he was safely on the tree he waved to Streak.

'Good luck, shipmate,' Streak yelled. 'Hoist the yard-arm and watch your back.'

'And good luck to you,' Joe called back.

With Judy at his heels, her tail wagging, he walked carefully along the trunk of the giant tree. The bark was dry and brittle and a couple of times his feet slipped, but he made it safely to the river bank. Then he spotted the toad. It was hopping slowly along the trunk towards them.

'Oh no,' he said to Judy. 'That's going to slow us down. We can't possibly take the toad.'

Judy looked at him, then at the toad. She ran back along the trunk to where the toad sat watching. Joe couldn't think why the toad would want to come.

*On my back, on my back*, Judy told the toad. To Joe's amazement the toad must have understood. It gave a loud, rasping croak and with one huge hop leapt on to the dog's back.

'Well I never,' Joe said, laughing. If the toad wanted to come along with them and Judy was happy to carry it, he had no objections.

He turned for one last look at the barge. Streak, in his red bandana, was perched on the rail of the boat. '*Bon voyage!*' he yelled. The other monkeys were waving.

Joe smiled and waved backed and then walked into the shadow of the trees.

The going was tough, especially at first. The undergrowth along the river's edge was a tangle of weeds and thistles. It soon thinned out, but not before Joe's bare feet were badly scratched and sore. The wood was peculiarly still, as though all the sounds from the outside had been muffled by its trees. Even the continuous chirping of birds and insects seemed muted. It was a strange sensation moving beneath the densely woven branches of the trees, almost bare for the winter, but with the dazzling light of the sun above. What was stranger still was finding the occasional tree still fully laden with leaves, as though the changing season had passed it by.

Most of the trees were silver birches, but taller than Joe had ever seen before, and scattered among them were a few oak and chestnut trees. Even the oak trees seemed thin and fragile, not like the majestic oaks that soared above the playing field near Joe's home. The wood was littered with fallen branches, most of which were covered with glutinous fungi and mould. The smell of decay hung heavy on the air. It was a dismal place.

Eventually they found a path. Suddenly Judy became excited.

*I've found it. Yes, this is it. Come on! Come on!*

Joe breathed a sigh of relief. At last Judy had picked up Hannah's scent.

'Not too fast,' Joe said. 'Just take it nice and steady. We mustn't get lost.'

Judy rushed along the path, stopped and came running back.

*This way. This way.*

Despite the knot of fear that had made its home in Joe's stomach, he chuckled. Judy looked so comical with the big warty toad balanced on her back.

Joe kept his eyes peeled for the creeper. If it was as dangerous as he'd been led to believe, he didn't want to be caught by surprise. Vines hung from the trees like thick cobwebs and after only a few minutes' walking they encountered some tendrils hanging down across the path. Joe was wary of touching them. Perhaps this was the creeper. But it seemed dead. Hesitantly he reached forward and touched it, half expecting it to wrap itself around his arm. But nothing happened. It seemed safe enough. He brushed it aside and it disintegrated in a cloud of dust. Joe coughed, wiping the dust from his eyes. He ran out of the way.

'Look, Judy,' he spluttered. 'I'm covered in it.'

*Come along, come along, it's only a little dust.*

'That's what I like about you,' Joe said. 'You're so sympathetic.'

The path wound through the shadows of the trees. There was something depressing about the wood, Joe thought. There was decay all around them, but this wasn't the normal decay of autumn. There was something unhealthy here but he couldn't quite put his finger on what it was. Twice they had to climb over fallen tree trunks that blocked their way. Once Joe paused to watch a huge black stag-beetle crawl out of an even blacker recess in the base of a tree and scuttle across his path. A little while later he saw a tortoise run by. A tortoise running? And how on earth had a tortoise got here?

They'd been walking for about an hour when they came to a clearing. For some time the path had been going uphill. Joe's legs ached, his feet hurt and he was thirsty. He called for a rest and sat on a black rock. The patch of blue sky above seemed so cheerful after the gloominess of the wood. Here the grass shone with an emerald brightness and there were pale green mushrooms growing every-where. He took a swig from his water-bottle, all the while watching out for the creeper. Joe peered up the path. The mountain was just visible above the tops of the trees. Hannah was somewhere ahead. And maybe even his father. That was something he didn't want to think about. If his father *was* there after all . . . Suddenly Judy started barking. She'd found something further up the path.

Joe stuffed the bottle back into his rucksack, slung it over his shoulders and made his way warily forward. He caught Judy up and stood and stared. There before them was a long line of hedgehogs, going round and round in a circle. Joe estimated the circle to be about twenty metres in diameter. Round and round the hedgehogs were going, each following the one in front.

'What do you make of that?' he asked Judy. 'They remind me of us. Going round in circles, not getting anywhere.'

Judy sniffed at one of the hedgehogs and growled.

'I don't think they'll hurt you,' Joe said.

The toad croaked.

Joe put a foot down in front of one of the hedgehogs.

'At least, I hope they're harmless.'

The hedgehogs came to an abrupt halt. Joe was half prepared for a vicious bite, but the hedgehog only sniffed at Joe's foot with its snout and began to crawl around it. The others followed.

Joe and Judy watched the procession make its way slowly into the undergrowth until it disappeared from view beneath the trees.

From somewhere ahead there was a scream followed by a shout.

'Help me – help!'

'It's Hannah!' Joe yelled. 'Come on!'

## CHAPTER 18

# CREEPER

Joe ran along the path towards the cry. Judy raced ahead, the toad clinging precariously to her back. After several minutes Joe reached the edge of the wood. A gentle slope of rock-strewn grass rose before him, stretching to the foot of the mountain, a huge rocky outcrop, rearing high above him, obscuring the sky. Joe came to a sudden halt at the sight that greeted him. Judy had stopped too. She was barking and growling, her teeth bared.

There were numerous low brick buildings clustered around the foot of the mountain and Joe could see a road winding through the maze of buildings, leading from a hole in the rock to a gate set in the high, barbed-wire fence around the perimeter. The gate hung open, broken. And there, in front of the gate, about fifty metres away, was Hannah. Surrounded by huge, white rats.

Joe stood and stared – at the huge complex of laboratories and at the rats, but most of all at Hannah. As if on some pre-arranged signal every rat turned to stare at Joe. He felt waves of hate coming from the hundreds of pale eyes that bored into him.

The rats had cut off any hope of Hannah escaping, or of Joe and Judy reaching her. Joe watched helplessly as the rats began to shepherd Hannah towards the gate. Then he saw the creeper. It was moving around each side of the rats and their captive, slithering down the side of the mountain and through the gate. It looked like a snake – many snakes. Each strand was the thickness of Joe's arm – and the snaky strands were now sliding effortlessly along the grass towards them, like a sea of slimy spaghetti. The creeper was a bright, unhealthy green, glistening in the sun.

Joe stood transfixed. The elusive memory of his earlier encounter with the creeper suddenly came back to him with crystal clarity. The skin on his leg, where the creeper had attacked him, began to itch unbearably. The strands of creeper were edging closer. He knew he must do something – but what? His legs were unbearably tired. He felt unable to move.

He could hear a murmuring sound in his ears, like distant voices singing. But the song had no melody – it was a cacophony of noise. He listened, trying to make sense of it.

*Don't be afraid. Come to us. Everything is all right.*

Now the strands of creeper, sliding smoothly along the ground, had almost reached him. Judy looked terrified. She was barking furiously and shaking violently, her tail between her legs. The toad was croaking piteously. Joe could picture the creeper wrapping itself around him, its touch wet and cold. He could picture it dragging him towards Hannah, to the mountain, into the mountain's dark core. For he knew now, with absolute certainty, that the creeper came from the mountain. But he couldn't move, didn't want to. The soothing voices lulled his mind.

Suddenly Hannah saw him. She screamed.

'Run! Run! Get away!'

Her voice broke through the noise in his head and he glanced up at her. The spell was broken. He turned and fled. He ran faster than he'd ever run before, his breath coming in ragged gulps, his back prickling with fear, his bare feet pounding on the hard earth of the path. Judy raced past him, the toad clinging to her back. He glanced over his shoulder.

Some of the rats had detached themselves from the main group and were chasing them. In no time Joe was back at the clearing, but he knew he couldn't run any further. And the rats had been gaining on him all the while. He'd have to make a stand. He grabbed a branch to defend himself but the wood crumbled in his hand. He threw it aside in disgust.

Joe stood in the centre of the clearing with Judy by his side as about thirty of the giant rats ran around them, until they, like Hannah, were surrounded. The rats made no move to attack them. Judy growled.

*Come on, then. Come and get it.*

Joe's breathing began to return to normal as he looked anxiously around, wondering what they could do. Why aren't they attacking? he wondered. The rats stood and stared at them, their eyes baleful and unblinking, as if waiting for some command. Then Joe understood.

'The creeper,' he said to Judy. 'They're waiting for the creeper. They must be under the creeper's control.'

And Hannah? Was she under the creeper's spell, too?

Had she lured him here for the creeper? He couldn't believe that was true. But he had no time to think about that now. They had to get away, before the creeper came.

'We'll have to fight them,' he told Judy. 'Once the creeper gets here we've had it.'

No sooner had he said this than Judy launched herself at the nearest rat and sank her teeth into its body. The rat squealed and wriggled, trying to get away. Several of the rats jumped on her. At that moment the toad spat at one of them. A globule of pink liquid hit the rat and it squealed in pain, falling on its side and writhing in agony.

'Here, Judy,' Joe commanded.

Judy shook a rat from her body, dislodging its sharp teeth, and rushed back to his side, panting and growling, her jaws teeth dripping saliva and blood. The encircling rats moved a little closer. How much time did they have? Joe wondered. He'd seen how fast the creeper could move. It would reach them any second.

Joe reached for the toad and gathered its soft, rough body gently in his hands. The toad allowed him to hold it.

'When I give the word,' he told Judy, 'we'll try and break through. We'll go back the way we came, towards the river.'

Joe took a deep breath. 'Now,' he yelled.

Again Judy tore into the rats, snapping at them wildly. At once the rats were upon her, a sea of snapping, hissing, bloated bodies. Joe joined her, kicking at the rodents with his feet, holding the toad like a gun. As the rats snapped at his legs the toad spat at them. Several fell beneath the scrambling bodies, hit by the toad's deadly poison. A searing stab of pain shot through Joe's body as a rat sank its teeth into his leg. The toad spat and the rat fell away, squealing in pain.

It was all over in minutes. Despite the overwhelming number of rats, they'd done it. Bodies of the dead and dying rats littered the ground around their feet.

'I can't believe it,' Joe said, out of breath again. 'We did it.'

Then he winced in pain. The rat bite on his leg was beginning to throb. In the fury of the battle he'd forgotten about the creeper. It would be here soon. They had to run, now.

He glanced quickly around but it was too late. The creeper was there. It had twisted and snaked its way all around the clearing. Joe looked wildly about for some way through, but there was none. And the voices in his head were starting again. It must only be a matter of seconds now before the creeper closed in for the kill.

## CHAPTER 19

# THE MOUNTAIN TRAIL

Joe sat on the black rock and fondled Judy's head. The toad had resumed its place on the dog's back. For several minutes Joe had stood nervously waiting for the creeper to attack, trying to look for some way through. But no attack came. He considered running at the creeper and trying to jump over it, but there was too much of it and more strands were arriving all the time, making the wall several metres deep. The voices in his head were less insistent now. Just a background noise, like the hiss of interference on the radio.

'What now, Judy? It's got us pinned down, but it isn't attacking. I wonder why?'

*I'm thirsty. It's thirsty work this rat business.*

'Me, too,' Joe said.

He unhitched his rucksack and took out his water-bottle. There was a dip in the surface of the rock and Joe poured a little water into it. Judy lapped it up noisily. He took a swig himself.

'Well, we can't stay here for ever,' he said. 'There must be some way through.'

But the prospects didn't look very good. Any moment now, he knew, the creeper could close in and that would be the end. And even if it stayed where it was, it could wait for hours or days or weeks and they would simply die of thirst or starvation. The water would soon run out and Joe hadn't brought anything to eat. The creeper might summon more rats, too. He looked around the clearing and noticed the mushrooms.

'I wonder if those mushrooms are edible?' he mused. 'Probably poisonous. They look unhealthy.'

He bent down and picked one. It came out of the ground easily. He examined it. It looked like a mushroom except for its green colour and size. It felt firmer than a normal mushroom, too. If it was edible it would be too tough to eat, Joe thought. He laid it on the rock. He'd pack it in his rucksack and have a better look at it later, when they escaped. He glanced up anxiously at the gathering strands of creeper. *If* they escaped.

Joe's leg was aching now. He rolled his trouser leg up to examine the bite. There were two rows of teeth marks, dotted with tiny spots of blood. Beneath the marks his leg was beginning to swell and a bruise was forming.

'I'll need a tetanus jab for that,' he said.

Joe was putting the water-bottle back in his rucksack when he noticed the Coke bottle. 'Of course,' he exclaimed, 'the creeper repellent.'

*The what?*

'The creeper repellent. Renaldo gave it to me. I'd forgotten all about it.'

Joe pulled the bottle out and examined it. 'Good old Renaldo. Maybe we've a chance after all.' He jumped

excitedly to his feet and slung the rucksack on his back.
'Let's try it.'

*Yes, try it. Let's try it.*

'We've nothing to lose, have we? Keep close, Judy.'

He noticed the mushroom still lying where he'd put it
on the rock. He grabbed it and stuffed it in his pocket.

'Are you ready?' he asked the dog.

*Yes, yes. Come on. What are we waiting for?*

Joe approached the creeper cautiously, holding the
Coke bottle out in front of him. Carefully he pulled out
the makeshift cork. He hoped this would work. But what
other choices did they have? Earlier he'd noticed another
path that led off to the left, running parallel with the
mountain, between two trees that formed an archway. He
decided that they would try that way. They had to rescue
Hannah, but he didn't relish the thought of going directly
towards the mountain and the rats. And, anyway, the
mountain was where the creeper seemed to originate
from.

As they neared the creeper the voices began again.

*Come with us. We mean you no harm. Be one with us. We will
give you power. Come. Join us.*

Joe closed his mind to the insistent voices. They were at
the creeper now. The slimy surface of the interwoven
strands glistened in the patches of sunlight. The creeper
began to move towards him. A tendril rose to meet him
like a cobra preparing to strike. It wavered in the air for a
second then lunged at him. The voices in his head were
now at fever pitch.

*Come with us. Join us. Be one of us.*

Joe shook the bottle at the creeper, showering it with

the liquid. There was a hissing sound as the tendril jerked back. The strands on the ground began to writhe as droplets of the liquid fell on them. Joe sprinkled more liquid on the mass of strands. He could hear screaming in his head. He sprinkled more. He'd already used most of the bottle. It seemed to be working, but would there be enough? Suddenly one of the strands broke. Then another. There was an awful smell, a cross between the scent of a bonfire and the stench of a compost heap. Furiously Joe emptied the bottle. The creeper's tendrils parted.

'Run!' Joe yelled.

From the corner of his eye he could see other strands of creeper moving around the outside to try to cut them off. Joe and Judy sprinted through the gap and along the path into the shelter of the trees. There was a terrible wailing sound in his head. He and Judy ran as fast as they could, through the dark wood, following the new path, until the voices had faded and they felt safe.

Joe slowed to a walk. He was covered in sweat and breathing heavily. We did it, he thought, we did it.

'Well done!' He patted Judy's head. She wagged her tail delightedly.

*We did it. We did it. The creeper doesn't scare us, does it? Oh no.*

Joe laughed with relief.

'If you say so,' he grinned.

The toad croaked.


As they walked in the shadow of the trees they could sense rather than see the mountain to their right. The dry heat of the day began to replace the damp coolness of the wood as the trees thinned. They passed a huge thicket of bamboo that towered high into the sky. Bamboo growing on the marsh? How on earth had that got here? Giant red butterflies fluttered around it. Not for the first time Joe wished he had his camera with him. Nobody would believe some of the plants and the creatures he had seen in this alien place. They could hear bird-song again. The path was veering to the right and here the gentle slope seemed to be levelling out.

They soon reached a clearing, a patch of high ground surrounded by brambles covered in ripe blackberries. Two huge black rocks reared before them. To their left the path led down through more woodland. But that way the trees looked normal, clad in the last remnants of autumn foliage. Healthy, too. They didn't have the decayed look of the trees in the dying wood that they'd been travelling through. And from here the mountain was in full view. Joe paused for a moment to look at it. Hannah had been right – this wasn't a real mountain. But it *was* huge. And it had an air of menace. Its rocky face loomed dark and sinister against the sky. A seagull wheeled overhead and its cry echoed off the black rock walls like a cry of pain.

He noticed two huge trees in the mountain's shadow. Their trunks were bent, no doubt by the wind, but their shape gave the impression that they were cowering before the mountain's presence, as though they desperately wanted to get away.

'What now, Judy?' Joe asked.

Joe picked a blackberry and popped it in his mouth. The fruit was sweet and sharp. It reminded him how hungry he was. His tummy rumbled. What he wouldn't give for a proper meal. He looked up. Several other seagulls had joined the first and the birds circled one another, climbing and gliding smoothly upon the warm air that rose from the sun-drenched rocks.

The path seemed to lead in the wrong direction, away from the mountain. Joe had to rescue Hannah, but there seemed no point in going back the way they'd come. Approaching the mountain from the front would be suicide, especially as the bottle of creeper repellent was empty. But he knew he had to free her from the creeper. And this raised a rather scary notion – that the creeper was intelligent.

Could a plant have intelligence? He remembered what Hannah had said. Had the scientists succeeded in producing intelligent plant life? Rats, he knew, were intelligent. But the rats seemed to be working *for* the creeper. But maybe not. Maybe the scientists had found some way to link the intelligence of the rats *with* the creeper. Whatever they'd done it was now out of control. Joe shivered. He didn't really want to think about that any more.

'Let's carry on for a bit,' Joe said to Judy. 'The path might lead us around the other side of the mountain.'

Joe picked a couple more blackberries and ate them.

'Come on, then,' he said. 'Let's go.'

*Yes, let's go. Let's go.*

Judy wasn't really a very stimulating conversationalist, but Joe was glad she was with him. She bounded down the path and disappeared from view into the trees. Joe followed, chewing the blackberries thoughtfully.

After a few minutes the wide path began to slope gently down. It was overgrown with weeds and grass but was not impassable and there weren't too many thistles and brambles to avoid. Joe's bare feet swished through the red and golden leaves and the noises of insect life and birds provided a pleasant background to his thoughts. He was thinking back to his conversations with Hannah. If only Hannah had told him all about this when they'd first met. But would he have helped her? Would he even have believed her? No, of course not. He'd have thought she was mad. For the first time he began to feel a little sympathy for her predicament.

The trees were now quite dense and it was cooler here, out of the heat of the sun. To his left was a high hedge of privet, covered in red Virginia creeper. Judy appeared, her tail wagging furiously.

*Come and see this. Come on.*

And she bounded off again.

Joe quickened his pace. What had Judy found now?

He turned a corner and the hedge and the trees ended abruptly. He was looking out across the marsh, spread before him like one of those aerial photographs you see taken from a plane. The ground sloped sharply away from the trees, down to the marsh, and he could see a river far below, sparkling in the sun. And beyond the river a high fence. Was it the same river, he wondered, that they'd travelled along with the monkeys? Probably not. And to the right he could see the sea. All he and Judy had to do was make their way down the hill, following the edge of the wood, until they reached the sea and they'd be free. But first he had to rescue Hannah and this route was obviously no good. It would take them even further from the rats and the creeper and their prisoner.

He looked around for Judy and gasped in surprise. Joe

had been so busy looking out across the marsh that he hadn't noticed where they were.

To his left, where the high hedge ended, was a cottage. The path led around a fence, also overgrown with Virginia creeper, blazing golden-red in the sun, to a gate. There the path gave way to a cart track that led down the hill, past several other houses.

Judy came rushing up to him.

*Civ . . . civ . . .*

Joe laughed. 'Civilization?'

*Yes, yes. Civ . . . civ . . .*

'I think you may be right,' Joe said excitedly. He'd had a thought. They would have a telephone in the cottage. He could phone for help. And he could phone home, tell his mum he was all right and find out if his dad had returned. 'Come on, Judy. Let's go and see.'

## CHAPTER 20

# THE COTTAGE

Joe stood at the cottage gate and felt his excitement ebbing away. As soon as he reached the gate, hanging open and entwined with vine, it became obvious that the building was deserted. A path, overgrown with buttercup and clover, led up to the front door and the garden was a riot of weeds. Only a few roses poked up above the mass of thistles, briars, dandelions and, most of all, long grass. The roses were covered in creeper but not, Joe was thankful, of the variety that held Hannah captive. But even in that mini-jungle the roses looked beautiful and their pink, red and white blooms filled the air with a delicious and distinctive scent. Bees buzzed around them, collecting the last of the season's pollen.

The cottage itself was dilapidated. Paint peeled from the white walls and the windows were boarded up. Joe looked anxiously around for phone lines, but there was none. He would not be able to phone home after all. Judy was at the front door, sniffing two empty milk bottles lying by the front step. Joe looked down the track. He could see that the other houses were deserted too. He sighed, and went to join Judy.

'Hello?' he called out.

*Hello!*

'Not you, Judy . . . Hello,' he called again. 'Is anyone there?'

Joe went up to the door and tried it. As he had expected, it was locked. He banged the knocker. Nothing. Only the sounds of insects and bees and birds in the trees. Joe noticed a path leading around the house. He remembered something Hannah had said. She had lived on the mountain. Had this cottage been her home, then? Was this where she was heading? Not to the mountain, but home?

'I'm going to have a look round the back,' Joe told Judy.

Cautiously he made his way around the side of the house. The path was narrow, and made more difficult by a clump of head-high nettles, but he managed to thread his way between them and the side of the house without being stung.

There was a tiny yard at the back where a high hedge and the trees cut out all the light. Whereas the front of the cottage had looked quite picturesque, although dilapidated, the back, couched in shadow, looked positively spooky. A row of sticks poked above the weeds in the garden. It must once have been a vegetable plot, Joe thought. He could see the top of what looked like a well. The grass around it was trampled down. He studied the back of the cottage. The windows here were also boarded up, but the back door was slightly ajar.

He looked round for Judy. She was still at the front

somewhere. 'Judy, Judy. Here, girl,' he called. Joe felt uneasy. There was something not quite right, and he wanted the dog by his side. Joe listened. He could hear something. The path carried on around the other side of the cottage but it was lost in a mass of overgrown hydrangea and clematis. Something was there. He could hear it moving through the greenery. Rats? Not more rats. He felt the familiar fear returning to the pit of his stomach.

'Judy! Quickly!' he yelled.

The bush was moving as whatever it was pushed its way through. A dark shape appeared and rushed towards him.

*Here I am. Here I am. What is it?*

Joe let out a huge sigh of relief. It was Judy.

'Why did you come that way?' he asked her as she ran up to him, panting. 'You scared the life out of me.'

*You called me. I came.*

'Yes, I know. I thought you were another rat.'

*A rat? How could you?* Judy seemed offended.

There was a croak and the toad appeared out of the undergrowth and hopped towards them.

'You must have knocked the toad off,' Joe said.

*I was in a hurry. You called me.*

The toad hopped up to Judy and resumed its place on her back.

'Looks like you found a real friend there,' Joe said. 'Let's look inside the cottage.'

Tentatively Joe pushed the back door and it creaked open. He peered in. It was dark and gloomy inside and the floor was covered in broken crockery and cutlery. Several drawers lay upturned on the floor and dead leaves rustled around them in the breeze.

Joe stared into the gloom. It looked like someone had been searching for something. He noticed something by his feet. A pair of wire clippers. Joe bent down and picked them up. They looked new and seemed out of place, somehow, in this old, deserted building.

'Come on,' Joe said. 'We're wasting our time. Let's go back.'

Joe paused at the garden gate to take a last look at the marsh spread before him, and the distant ocean and freedom, then he turned his back on it and made his way quickly past the high hedge of privet and Virginia creeper, retracing his steps through the silver birches, towards the mountain and the nightmare he had so recently left.

They were soon back at the clearing. Judy lay down, panting, her front legs crossed before her, and Joe stared at the mountain, getting his breath back from the climb, and thinking. They had to rescue Hannah – and soon. It might already be too late. But he still had no idea how they were going to do it. If only there was some other way on to the mountain. He looked at the two slabs of black rock. There seemed to be a gap between them. Perhaps there was a way through. He walked across the clearing to investigate.

'Come on, Judy,' he said. 'Let's see if there's a way through here.'

He squeezed himself between the two huge slabs of granite and then stopped dead, just in time. For there before him stretched the sea, glistening in the sun, but below him was a vertical drop to a rocky beach, far below. He experienced a momentary wave of vertigo. It was a *long* way down.

It was quite a view. The sea breeze blew in his face and

the cries of seagulls drifted overhead. He could hear the surf crashing lazily along the shoreline, but before he had time to really appreciate the beauty of the scene, Judy rushed past him.

'Wait!' he yelled. But it was too late. Judy and the toad disappeared over the edge.

# CHAPTER 21

# ON THE BEACH

'No!' Joe cried. His heart went to his mouth and he experienced a second wave of dizziness. He hardly dared to look down. He couldn't face the sight of Judy lying dead on the rocks below. What was he going to do now? A wave of panic gripped him. He took several deep breaths and it subsided. There was no point in panicking. He had to do something. But what?

*Come on. Come on. What are you waiting for?*

Joe was hearing voices again. But no – he wasn't. It was Judy. Cautiously he peered over the edge of the cliff. Just below him was a ledge and there was Judy, the toad still clinging to her back. She was looking up at him with her big brown eyes and her tail was wagging. A wave of relief swept through him and he grinned at the dog. She was safe.

*Are you coming or what?*

An overgrown path zigzagged down the side of the cliff to the beach. Gingerly Joe climbed over the edge, clinging to the long grass along the cliff top, and lowered himself down on to the ledge. He gave Judy a great big hug.

'I'm so glad you're OK,' he said, tears in his eyes. 'I thought I'd lost you.'

The toad croaked.

'You, too,' he told the toad.

Joe wasn't very good with heights. He tried not to look down. He had a choice now. They could go back or go down to the sea. Joe needed time to think. There was no point going back until he had a plan and right now he couldn't think of any way to beat the creeper. It was possible there was a way round the mountain from the beach, perhaps at low tide. He made up his mind. They would go down.

Carefully they negotiated the climb down the cliff. It wasn't as difficult as it had looked. The path was fairly wide and as they neared the bottom it became easier, as well as less frightening.

At last they were at the foot of the cliffs. Joe stared up, hardly believing that just a few minutes ago they had been at the top. To his left the cliffs gave way to the mountain which jutted out into the sea, forming a headland. To his right the cliffs stretched into the distance.

In the shelter of the cliffs, where the sea had piled up the shingle against the chalky white face, the breeze had dropped and he could feel the warmth of the late-afternoon sun overhead. The tiny pebbles felt dry and warm beneath his bare feet. He turned and gazed across the beach at the waves gently rolling in. The sea looked cool and inviting.

'Come on, Judy,' he said and he ran towards the ocean.

The shingle gave way to sand. Joe dodged between the great clumps of brown seaweed, like knotted spaghetti, thrown up by the sea. His foot landed on one and a cloud of tiny flies erupted into the air. But in no time Joe was at the water's edge. He unslung his rucksack, flinging it back across the sand to land with a thump. Then, whooping with delight, he splashed into the sea.

Joe ran along the shoreline, laughing, weaving in and out of the breaking waves and swirling foam, kicking through the icy-cold water with his bare feet. Judy raced around him, barking madly, rolling in the wet sand and the smelly seaweed, leaping the waves. With the cry of the seagulls above, the cool breeze in his face and the ocean's pounding song, Joe let himself forget about the last few days, about the deadly creeper and about Hannah's plight, and simply splashed about happily. For the moment he felt gloriously free of all his worries. Laughing joyfully, he kicked water at Judy.

*Watch it! Watch it!* Judy barked playfully.

The toad began to croak. Joe was unsure whether the toad was enjoying the game or complaining. He decided to call a halt. He didn't want to upset the toad. He could do without it spitting poison at him.

He walked out of the water and collapsed on the hot sand, out of breath. Judy ran across to him and shook herself, spraying water everywhere. It was all too much for the toad who leapt off Judy's back with a disdainful croak and hopped across the sand towards the cliffs, coming to rest in the shadow of a large rock.

Joe laughed and rubbed his hands along Judy's back and sides and hugged her.

'You're all wet,' he said, 'and I don't care.'

Joe stared at the mountain, its sheer black walls a stark

contrast to the white chalk of the cliff face. The rocks that littered the beach around its base reminded Joe of Plasticine, as though a giant had moulded them with his huge thumbs.

There must be a way to free Hannah, he thought. Then something caught his eye. It looked like a large boat, caught up on the rocks where the mountain met the sea. He stood up for a better view. It was a wreck of some kind. As he walked towards it, a sense of foreboding gripped him. He recognized it. He knew what it was. It was the barge.

And it lay wrecked on the rocks.

## CHAPTER 22

# THE WRECK

Joe felt devastated. He looked anxiously around for any sign of the monkeys. But there was none. Had they perished, then? Had they all drowned? Despair gripped him. The tide was coming in and he could see no way of reaching the wrecked barge. It was getting dark, too. By now the sun had disappeared behind the cliffs, the sky was turning pink and the air was cooling.

All he could do was find somewhere sheltered to sleep and start again in the morning. He retrieved his rucksack and trudged wearily up the beach. He found a small cave in the cliff face in which he could shelter from the salty breeze, and pulled out his sleeping-bag.

As he lay looking up at the sky, watching the first few stars twinkle into view, Joe thought about the monkeys. They couldn't all have died, could they? He thought about Hannah, captured by the rats and the creeper. Where was she now? Was she still alive? If she was, she would be waiting for him to come and rescue her. He was hungry and thirsty, too. What he wouldn't give now for a nice plate of boiled fish.

He cuddled Judy. 'Don't worry,' he told her. 'It will all be all right tomorrow.'

*Yes, yes. Tomorrow. We'll find a juicy bone.*

Joe fell asleep and he dreamed of Streak and Hannah, walking hand in hand up the path to his front door. The door opened and there was his dad, safe and sound. But his father had the face of a rat.

In the morning Joe set out to investigate the barge. The sky was overcast and a chill wind blew from the sea. Judy followed him as he made his way towards the mountain and the wreck. The mountain looked somehow desolate this morning, almost insubstantial. The silky sand was flat and damp, littered with pebbles and tiny pink shells. There were breathing holes and casts made by lugworms everywhere. Joe wished he still had his fishing-rod. How nice it would be to be digging bait, ready for a day's fishing, rather than having to worry about the creeper and the danger he would soon have to face.

As well as the casts and air holes, there were larger indentations in the sand, each the size of a 2p coin. Joe wondered what could have made them. There were brown ribbons of the spaghetti-like seaweed, too, scattered all around. The seaweed, with its twisty shapes, reminded Joe of Chinese writing. Then he stopped and stared at the strands around his feet. The strands seemed to have arranged themselves into a word – *Help*. Surely not. Joe's mouth was suddenly dry and he felt his heart beating. He looked again. No, it was his imagination. It was just seaweed after all, scattered in random shapes.

Joe took a deep breath and walked on. The tide was out,

leaving the wreck beached. They climbed over the lichen-covered rocks and skirted the deeper pools until they reached the barge. The barge's brass ladder jutted out of the sand like a weird piece of sculpture. After several tries Joe managed to clamber aboard.

The deck was more or less intact but there was wreckage everywhere, and no sign of the monkeys. Joe looked at the devastation and sighed, but all the while he was thinking of Hannah caught in the tendrils of the creeper. He could still picture the last time he'd seen her, surrounded by all those evil-looking rats. He half expected that at any minute the rats would come swarming down the mountain to get him. And he was still no nearer a solution to his problem. How on earth could he rescue her? He could do with a few gallons of the creeper repellent that Renaldo had made, but it would take days to find Renaldo, especially as they no longer had a boat. And he had no idea how the stuff was made or he'd make some himself.

From where he stood, Joe had a different view of the mountain. Perhaps there was another way in? Well, he would have to look. There was no point standing staring into space. He swung himself over the edge of the barge and dropped to the beach, landing in a shallow pool with a squelch.

'Come on,' he called Judy, 'Let's take a walk.'

*Yes, yes, a walk — let's take a walk.*

They made their way around the headland. After about a hundred metres or so the mountain curved back towards the cliff. The beach was very rocky here. Judy followed Joe as he threaded his way through the seaweed and between the black rocks, some taller than he was. She sniffed at anything which might be edible.

Joe stopped to peer into a rock pool. He was reminded of a holiday he'd spent with his mum and dad several years ago. The weather was similar to this, cold and grey, although it had been in the middle of August rather than October. His mother had never liked the cold and had sat huddled up in her coat on a deck-chair while he and his father had hunted for crabs in rock pools.

He thought of his father again. He had long ago decided that he wasn't on the marsh, but still the nagging feeling wouldn't go away. What if he *was* here somewhere? What if he had been captured by the creeper? He'd questioned Judy further about the man she'd claimed to have seen, but the dog had been very vague and the conversation had led nowhere. If his father was here, it was all the more imperative to get into the mountain. But it all seemed somehow remote, now. His escapades on the marsh seemed more like a dream. Did it really happen? Joe was beginning to have doubts. Then he saw something. A cave.

There was a dark opening between three massive rocks that stood like sentinels guarding the entrance. He called to Judy, who was tugging at a bit of driftwood half buried in the sand.

Carefully he picked his way across the shingle and around the sharp rocks and pools until he stood between the three huge black rocks. It was a cave all right. But how far back did it go? He stepped through the narrow entrance. It was dark inside and he waited for his eyes to become adjusted to the gloom. The roof was just above his head, but the cave was quite wide and it seemed to go back into the mountain. Before him stretched a pool of water. If he went any further into the cave he'd have to wade through it.

He could hear the wind whistling past the cave mouth and the drip of water up ahead. He could smell the saltiness of the sea mixed in with the damper, darker scent of stale air.

'Hello,' he called.

Hello – the muffled echo greeted him.

*Hello.*

Joe bent and ruffled Judy's fur.

'Don't start that again,' he said, smiling. 'Come on, let's go a little further in. Maybe it leads somewhere.'

He rolled his jeans up above his knees and took a tentative step into the cold water. His feet sank a little way into sand but the floor was firm. Slowly he and Judy edged their way into the darkness.

Joe held his arm out ahead of him, in case they met the back of the cave. It was pitch black now and he didn't want to collide with a rock. He felt something touch his hair and he stopped. He reached up. It was the roof of the cave getting lower. He felt out to the sides with his hands. His left hand touched something cold and slimy. Rock.

Joe took a couple more steps and felt around again. Yes, he could feel the cave narrowing on both sides, becoming funnel-shaped. Here the ground seemed to be sloping up and he was walking out of the water. He reached up – thin air. He felt sure now that the cave went somewhere. But he needed light. He still had some matches left but they were in his rucksack on the beach. He'd intended to go back for

149

it after he'd examined the wreck. He decided to go back for it now. It would be a good idea to bring the toad, too, if they could find it. He hadn't seen it since it hopped off Judy's back the day before. The toad would be useful if they met any rats.

'We're going back,' Joe told the dog.

*Yes, yes. Let's go back. I don't like it.*

The return journey was easier. Ahead he could see the pale light of the cave mouth. Judy swam before him, splashing through the water. Was it his imagination or was the water deeper than before? It was above his knees, soaking his turned-up jeans. A wave rolled past him, soaking him even more. Wading through the water was becoming much more of an effort. Then it dawned on him what was happening. The tide was coming in. He could clearly hear the crashing of the sea now, as it met the rocks around the entrance. They would have to be quick or they'd be cut off.

'Hurry,' he shouted to Judy.

He'd only taken a few more steps when he realized that the water was well above his knees, soaking his jeans. Then he knew it was too late. Even if they made it to the entrance they would be cut off. He remembered the tide coming in the day before when he'd spotted the wrecked barge. With the sea pounding the headland and all those rocks, there was no way they would escape. Trying to swim against all the currents that would be created would be suicidal. There was only one thing they could do. They would have to go back and hope that the cave really did lead somewhere.

They retraced their steps, the sea now up to Joe's waist,

until at last they reached the back of the cave. Joe pulled himself from the water and stood shivering in the darkness. He heard Judy behind him. She shook herself violently and showered him with cold water.

'Thanks, Judy,' he said.

*What did I do? What did I do?*

'Nothing.'

Joe squatted in the darkness, shivering as dribbles of icy-cold water ran down his legs. He reached for Judy. Her coat was wringing wet.

'If only we had some light,' he muttered. 'Come on, let's see if this goes anywhere.'

A cool draught of air blew from the darkness behind them. Joe stood and took a few hesitant steps forward. The sand beneath his feet gave way to rock, cold and hard. He reached out to feel the walls of the cave. They were dry. He took a few more steps. The floor rose sharply. He felt above his head. Nothing. So far so good. Even if this cave went nowhere, he figured, it should at least provide a safe place to stay until the tide went back out. Provided, of course, that the cave itself didn't fill up with water.

They needed light. Perhaps his matches weren't in his rucksack. He wasn't sure. He could have put them in his pocket. He reached into his wet jeans to look and his hands closed on something soft. The mushroom. He'd forgotten all about that. He pulled it out. At once the cave was lit with a pale green light.

Joe stared at the mushroom in disbelief. It was glowing.

'Amazing,' he said.

Then a thought struck him. What if the mushroom was radioactive? Why else would it glow? If it was radioactive it could be incredibly dangerous – even deadly. What should he do? They needed the light, but what if the mushroom was giving out harmful rays? Well, he'd been carrying it around since yesterday. There was no point worrying about that now. If it was harmful, the damage would already have been done and a few more hours wouldn't make much difference, would it?

Joe looked around the cave.

'Wow,' he gasped. The cave did indeed go somewhere. Ahead of them steps had been cut into the rock.

'Who could have done that? Smugglers?' His dad had often told him tales of smugglers along this coast.

'I wonder where the steps lead,' he said to Judy.

*I wonder, too.*

They began to climb, their way lit by the dim glow of the mushroom. The sound of the sea crashing into the cave behind them grew fainter and Joe could hear Judy panting along behind him. After a few minutes' climb Joe stopped for a rest.

'Look at that,' he said to Judy.

There were strange white markings on the wall.

'It's some kind of writing. Maybe a secret code or ancient instructions written by smugglers a hundred years ago.'

He bent forward to read it in the ghostly light of the mushroom.

*Terry loves Julie. True.*

'Hmm,' Joe said. So he and Judy weren't the only ones to have discovered these steps. They continued climbing. Joe was thinking about Terry and Julie, wondering who they were. Certainly not smugglers. There was a turning ahead, and something trailing round the corner and down the steps a few paces before them. Joe knew what it was.

'Stop,' he whispered to Judy. 'Creeper!'

## CHAPTER 23

# THE PIT

Joe walked slowly forward towards the creeper trailing down the steps. It looked dead. He nudged it hesitantly with his foot. Nothing happened. Joe breathed a sigh of relief.

'It's dead all right.'

Judy followed him up the last couple of steps as they turned the corner. They were in another, larger, cave.

The roof of the cave was high and above them they could see thousands of bats clinging to it. Joe looked around. There was a rich, nauseating smell. The floor was covered with bat droppings. Joe shivered. He hoped the bats weren't hostile. To their left the passageway continued upwards.

'Let's go on,' Joe whispered very quietly. He didn't want to wake the bats up.

Cautiously they followed the trail of dead creeper up the steps. The light emitted by the mushroom gave the narrow tunnel a weird, unearthly quality. He half expected the creeper to come alive at any moment. The strands of creeper took up a lot of room in the tunnel, making negotiating the steps quite tricky.

Soon, though, the steps stopped and the tunnel levelled out into a much wider cave. Joe judged they must be level with the top of the cliff. As far as he could tell they seemed to be walking away from the sea and in the direction of the buildings on the other side of the mountain, where he had last seen Hannah surrounded by the ferocious white rats.

Joe stopped to listen. The silence was heavy and complete. All he could hear were his own heart thumping and Judy panting. He was listening for the sound of rats, but there could be anything ahead. Who knew what other terrifying creatures might live in the deep, dark recesses of the mountain?

The strands of creeper meandered along the cave floor and disappeared around a corner. It was hard to see very far ahead – the mushroom only gave out a small amount of light and its eerie glow was not enough to penetrate the furthest corners of the cave. Instead it cast its own dark shadows.

Joe stood for several minutes, plucking up the courage to go on. If they came upon the live creeper, he still had no idea what they could do. But he felt sure that Hannah was somewhere ahead and he knew they had to continue. If they could only get through the mountain without the creeper being aware of them, if they could at least get an idea of the lie of the land, then they could come back prepared.

Joe took a few steps forward. But Judy stayed where she was and made a quiet whimpering noise. Joe turned back. She was standing staring at him, her big brown eyes a ghastly green in the mushroom's light, her tail between her legs.

'What's up, Judy?' Joe whispered.

*I can smell it. I can smell it.*

Joe felt the tiny hairs on the back of his neck stand on end.

'What can you smell?' he whispered.

*I don't know – but it's bad. Let's go back. I found a good stick on the beach. It's a fine stick, oh yes. It's a fine stick for throwing.*

Joe went to Judy, crouched down and put his arm around her damp fur. She was trembling. He understood how she felt. He, too, wanted to turn back. Turning back would be an easy thing to do. But he had to go on. There were some things, he knew, that you had to do – however scared you felt.

'It will be all right,' he whispered bravely. 'Just follow me. I need you, you know. I can't do this on my own.'

The dog gave another little whimper and nuzzled her head against his.

*I'll follow. Judy will follow. I'm a brave girl. The creeper doesn't scare me . . .*

'That's my Judy,' Joe said, standing up.

*. . . much.*

Joe grinned despite himself. Well, it does scare me, he thought. He walked slowly to the corner and peeped round it. He could see nothing but blackness.

Tentatively he held up the mushroom. They were standing in the entrance of another large cave. Joe could smell it now, the smell of decay, the smell of death. Joe strained his eyes to see more, but the dim light was not enough to penetrate far. He became suddenly aware of the mountain's presence, like a great weight all around him, as though any minute the tons and tons of rock might collapse and bury him, crushing him and Judy into oblivion. He shuddered. Best try not to think about that.

Joe's eyes followed the line of creeper which disappeared into the gloom. The creeper skirted a dark shadow some way ahead on the floor of the cave. He tried to see what it was, but he was too far away.

'Come on,' he whispered very quietly to Judy. Slowly they crept forward, Joe's bare feet silent on the cold rock floor of the cave. The dark shadow revealed a hole. Joe held the mushroom above it, and found himself looking down into a pit. It was full of bones, gleaming eerily, pale green in the mushroom's light. Joe recoiled. He closed his eyes and took several deep breaths. He steadied himself and peered down again, half expecting to see the pit full of skeletons, moving, shuffling in the darkness below. But no – they were animal bones, he was sure. He felt sick. It was too much. He moved away from the edge.

What was that? He'd heard something – a faint sound. Joe strained his ears. It was a voice.

'Joe.'

He heard his name being called from the darkness ahead, so faint that he could barely hear it. Was his imagination playing tricks on him? But no, there it was again.

'Joe.'

This time it was a little louder. He recognized the voice. It was Hannah. She was safe. He felt a wave of relief. Followed by fear. He could hear something else, too. Another voice. A voice in his head.

*Come*, it said, *don't be afraid. We have been waiting for you.*

But he *was* afraid. What should he do? He was seized by indecision. Hannah was there – but so was the creeper. What did it want of him? He knew he ought to turn and run, to leave this nightmare behind him, as quickly as possible. Forget about the creeper. Run. Forget about the mountain. Run. Forget about the marsh. Just get the hell out of here. Forget about Hannah. No, he couldn't do that. Hannah was somewhere ahead. Slowly, almost against his will, he walked forward, following the strands of dead creeper into the darkness, trying not to think about the pit full of bones.

He could hear Judy behind him. She was still making whimpering noises, but she hadn't deserted him. He wouldn't blame her if she high-tailed it. She brushed against his legs, making him jump. He reached down and patted her.

'It's OK,' he whispered encouragingly.

All Joe's senses were alert as he crept towards yet another cave entrance, still following the trail of dead creeper.

'Joe!' There was Hannah's voice again. 'Joe, help.'

*Come, human, come. Not far now. We will not hurt you. There is nothing to fear.*

They were at the entrance now. Joe took a big breath to try to calm his jangling nerves. Then he walked through the opening in the rock. They were in a corridor, bending round to the right, and there was light ahead. Light in the middle of the mountain? How could that be? Had they passed through the mountain already? Were they about to come out the other side? As he and Judy slowly followed the winding tunnel the light became stronger.

*Not far now*, the voice wheedled, *just a few more steps and into the light.*

They turned a sharp corner and bright light blazed from a doorway ahead. Slowly, as though in a dream, Joe felt his body walking to the light. It was as if he had no control over his actions. One foot followed the other and, as though in a trance, he walked through the opening.

He gasped in surprise. For a moment he thought he might faint. He took several more stumbling steps. He could hear the soft swish of creeper sliding around the walls behind him. He knew now that there could be no turning back.

It was almost too much to take in at once. Joe, with Judy beside him, stood staring around the huge cavern. Unlike the other caves, it was obvious that this one was man-made. The light came from neon strips running along the high ceiling. The walls were smooth and cut square, the floor was dusty concrete. Along the walls to his right there were several small white buildings, their windows barred and their doors hanging open. All around he could see cages set into the walls and far away on the opposite wall a large doorway, its heavy iron door lying broken on the ground. He could see daylight flooding through the door, but he knew he had no hope of reaching it, for everywhere he looked he could see the creeper, twisting around the walls, around the cages, and across the floor.

Joe glanced round. Thick strands of creeper had moved behind them, cutting off their line of retreat. There was nothing else to do but to go forward.

'Joe, help me, help me.'

It was Hannah's voice. He glanced anxiously around, trying to see where her voice was coming from.

*Yes, human, help your friend. Come and see us. We are waiting. We have something for you.*

Joe could hear the other voices again. The meaningless sea of babblings and whisperings, like a thousand frightened animals lost on some ghostly ocean. Siren songs and wailings and moanings. A great soup of emotions, growing louder now, filling Joe's head. Joe tried to shut the noise out, tried to control his thoughts, tried to think, but it was no use.

The creeper coiled and slithered and snaked everywhere. But it made no move to attack. And ahead of them was a clear path, leading to the largest of the buildings. Joe, followed by Judy, walked anxiously along it. Joe hadn't noticed it before, but in the centre of the massive artificial cavern was a pool of water. It was probably thirty metres across, and the pathway, cleared by the creepers, passed by it. As they got closer the smell from the pool hit Joe's nostrils. It was a rank, fetid smell. It reminded Joe of lots of things at once. Of decay, of rotting meat, of the zoo, of compost heaps.

As they approached the pool Joe stopped in his tracks. A huge strand of creeper, the thickness of Joe's body, rose from the pool and trailed along the floor into the large building. The tendril's surface, a slick mottled green, glistened in the neon lighting. Then Joe noticed a series of troughs cut into the floor, leading from the cages into the pool. He shuddered. Whatever was in the dank, evil-smelling pool was not water. Whatever it was, Joe didn't want to think about it.

He passed by the pool, gingerly stepping over the troughs. They were stained a nasty brown colour.

'Joe, up here!'

Joe's eyes followed the line of the gullies up the gently sloping floor to the wall of the cave. Then he saw her. She was imprisoned in one of the cages.

'Don't worry,' he yelled. 'It's OK. We'll get you out.'

He tried to sound confident, reassuring, but he knew it was no use. The floor of the cave between himself and Hannah was covered by the creeper.

He heard the creeper moving behind them, closing in, forcing them further along the clear pathway. The cacophony of noise in his head began to grow in intensity. Now he and Judy were at the door to the building. It was dark inside. He did not want to go in but he knew he had no choice. Inside, he knew, was the heart of the creeper. The malevolent being that terrorized the marsh.

The voices in his head became a frenzy. He edged by the giant tendril, took a deep breath, and stepped in.

## CHAPTER 24

# SHOWDOWN

As Joe stepped into the building the wailing voices abruptly stopped. He eased himself carefully past the tendril and into the gloomy interior. It was a large room that must once have been the main laboratory. The benches which lined the walls were covered in scientific apparatus. Old-fashioned computers, like big grey boxes, sat forlornly on desks, covered in dust, and several chairs lay overturned on the tiled floor. But Joe hardly noticed any of this, for there ahead of him, in the centre of the room, was the most grotesque thing he had ever seen.

It was like a huge tuber, dark green and slimy. It seemed to fill the room with its evil presence. The thick tendril from the pool led into its middle and other, thinner creepers grew from its base, like the roots of a tree, spreading fan-like across the floor, winding around the stuff on the benches and disappearing out of the broken windows. There were broken and twisted metal bars around the tuber, interwoven with the thinner creepers coming from the ghastly plant's base and the floor was covered in broken glass. There must once have been some kind of box or cage that had constrained the thing.

Joe's mouth was dry and he could hear his heart thumping madly in his chest. Then he noticed a complicated mass of coloured wires leading from the tuber towards the back of the room. There, he could just make out two red eyes, staring back from the gloom. As his eyes became accustomed to the darkness, he could finally make out what it was. It was a rat. The creeper was attached to a rat, held immobile in some kind of apparatus. But it was no ordinary rat. It was all black, not unlike the one that Judy had thrown from the boat, but it was bigger, much bigger.

Joe looked back at the tuber. In its centre was a large gaping hole, like a mouth, and a dark green sap dripped from it like saliva. But the mouth didn't speak. The words came to Joe in his mind.

*Put the mushroom down,* the voice commanded. *You have no need of light.*

Joe looked around, desperately seeking some means of escape, but there was none. What could he do. Maybe he should try and reach the rat. Was the rat controlling the creeper or was it the other way round? No, it must be the rat. It was the rat, then, via the creeper, controlling all the other rats. That was it – he had to reach the rat, he had to kill it, but there was no way past the creeper.

*Put it down,* the voice said.

Joe felt sick. The scientists had found a way to combine the intelligence of the rat with the power of the creeper. Now the rat was conducting its own experiment and he and Hannah were to be its next subjects.

'What do you want?'

*You*, the voice said.

Joe felt a chill go up his spine.

'What do you mean?'

*You and the girl. You are going to join us. We need your strength. We need your young blood, your young juices. You are not the first. Already we have the power of words. We are new. We are powerful. And with you, the marsh will finally be ours.*

Not the first? His father? Had the creeper killed his father? Joe thought suddenly of the pit full of bones and of the pool of liquid outside, with the channels running down to it from the cages in the wall. The room began to spin. His father – not his father.

*Don't be scared*, said the voice in his head. *It won't hurt. You will join the other human soon. But first put the mushroom down.*

Joe felt close to panic now. So he would join Hannah in that cage. He thought again of the gullies running from the cages to the huge pool. It was the pool, then, that held the genes, the essence of the animals that the creeper and the rats had captured, and of the laboratory animals that hadn't managed to escape. And it was the pool that must be polluting and contaminating the marsh.

Joe glanced behind him. Maybe he and Judy could make a run for it. After all, they could move much faster than the creeper. They could go back the way they'd come. But he still had to rescue Hannah. He glanced round. His way was barred by the creeper. It was impossible. It was hopeless.

He turned to face the monstrous tuber again.

Then a thought struck him. Here he and Judy were, surrounded by the creeper and yet . . . the creeper hadn't attacked him. It could move in and kill him. It could do whatever it wanted. But it hadn't. Why not? What was it waiting for? And why had it brought him here? Why hadn't it simply shepherded him straight up to the cage? Something the creeper had said . . . what was it? He tried to think but the answer wouldn't come.

*The mushroom.*

And why did it keep mentioning the mushroom? Then he realized that it was Judy now speaking to him, not the tuber. What did Judy mean? Joe looked stupidly at the mushroom in his hand.

*It's scared of the mushroom.*

He looked around. Was that it? Then he could feel his grip on the mushroom begin to loosen, as though the creeper was somehow forcing his hand open, forcing him to drop it.

'Joe!' He heard Hannah's voice from the cage outside. She was shouting something. He strained to hear. 'The repellent,' she was yelling, 'the creeper repellent! Use it!'

'It's all gone,' Joe yelled back.

*Then use the mushroom!*

'Use it? How?

*No*, the voice said. *We are scared of nothing. Throw it away. We can give you power. Become one of us. Be a part of us. You will be strong, invincible. The marsh will be yours.*

Suddenly Judy was barking furiously. Joe felt a searing pain in the back of his leg. He looked round. There were rats pouring into the room. He looked at the evil, twisted root before him and hurled the mushroom into its gaping mouth.

All hell broke loose.

The voice in his head turned to a deafening wail of pain

and the creepers in the room began moving, at first slowly but then faster, wilder, as though out of control.

For a moment Joe stood and stared, as though pinned to the spot. A rat climbed his body. He shook it off and dived across the room, dodging a strand of creeper that came writhing at his head. He had spotted a closed door at the back of the room. He prayed it would be open. He turned the handle and yanked. It was a large cupboard, full of boxes. He squeezed in and pulled the door closed. Then he remembered Judy. She was still in the room.

Heavily outnumbered, Judy was fighting the rats as best she could. She killed one and then another with her strong jaws, but they were all over her, frenziedly biting her. And all the time the creeper was flailing around her.

'Judy! Here! Judy!' Joe screamed from the cupboard. Judy shook the rats off and bounded across the room to join him. He hugged Judy to him. She was shaking and whimpering from pain and fear. A tendril had fallen across the doorway making it impossible to close. Joe braced himself for another attack.

Now the rats seemed to lose all interest in Judy and began attacking one another. The creeper was out of control, too. Its snake-like arms were thrashing about wildly. One of the old computers crashed to the floor, sending splintered glass and dust everywhere. The wailing noise started up in Joe's head again. He clamped his hands over his ears, but it made no difference. He crouched down in the corner of the cupboard, trying to escape the noise thundering through his head.

And then it was all over. With a last groan, a final great spasm and a sigh, the creeper stopped moving. The noise inside Joe's head stopped. And the last few rats left alive fled out of the doorway.

Silence.

Groggily Joe got to his feet and peered through the dust motes that swirled in the air.

'Joe!' It was Hannah's voice. 'What happened?'

Joe picked his way across the debris in the room. The huge tuber, the heart of the creeper, had changed. It looked as though it had rotted. Now it was an oozy green mess and the tendrils that trailed from it looked lifeless, dead. The rat, attached to the tuber by wires, was dead too. In a way Joe felt sorry for it. None of this had been the rat's fault.

Joe stepped out into the vast cave and looked around. There was no sign of the rats and the creeper that covered the floor lay still.

'You did it! You did it!' Hannah was yelling from her cage with delight. 'You did it! You killed the creeper!'

Joe sighed. Had he? Had he killed the creeper? It certainly looked like it.

He made his way towards her, stepping over strands of the grey, unmoving creeper.

'I did, didn't I?'

Joe grinned. He took a deep breath, letting his body return to normal. He was still shaking and he felt sick. He began to laugh. Hannah was laughing, too.

Then Joe remembered Judy.

'Here, Judy,' he called. 'Here, girl. It's all right. It's safe now. The creeper's dead and the rats have gone. Come on.'

Hesitantly, Judy poked her head out from the doorway of the laboratory.

167

'Up here,' Joe called. 'Come on.' Judy sniffed at a strand of dead creeper and gave a little bark. Then she limped across the creeper-strewn floor towards them.

'How am I going to get out of here?' Hannah asked.

Joe kicked away a strand of creeper and opened the cage door. 'It wasn't locked.'

Hannah laughed with relief. 'Stupid of me,' she said. 'Of course not.'

They hugged one another. Judy arrived, her tail wagging. Joe bent down and Judy nuzzled her face into his and she licked him.

'It's OK, Judy,' he whispered. 'It's all right now. We did it. What a team!'

*A team, yes, a team.*

He inspected her for bites. There were several on her body and her legs, but they didn't seem too bad. They would have to get her to a vet, though. If any of the wounds turned septic they could be dangerous.

'Come on,' Joe said, standing. 'Let's get out of here.'

'OK,' Hannah said. 'But there's something I have to get first.'

CHAPTER 25

# HANNAH'S SECRET

Joe and Hannah stood outside the cave mouth, staring down across the buildings of the complex and out over the marsh beyond the high fence. The weather was grey and miserable and there was a chill in the air. Now the euphoria that Joe had felt when the creeper had died was seeping away. He was thinking back over all the remarkable things that had happened in the last few days. How long had he been on the marsh? He'd lost all track of time. And he hadn't found his father. Had his father been here? Had the creeper caught him? Were his father's bones in that awful pit? He shivered at the thought. The creeper must have caught someone – or it wouldn't have been able to speak to him in his own language. Or would it?

'I wonder what will happen now that the creeper is dead?' Joe said.

Hannah shrugged. 'I expect the marsh will return to normal – eventually.'

There was a bang. Joe jumped. But it was only one of the large doors to the cavern being slammed shut by the wind. A large sign had fallen from it. It said *Government*

*Research Laboratories. No Admittance to Unauthorized Person-nel.* He thought about the scientists who had worked here, tampering with the way plants and animals grew. Was this some sort of government project that had got out of control? He'd probably never know. He remembered the cages in the cavern, the pit and the pool, and he shuddered. Well, whatever it was, he thought, it wasn't going on any longer.

Joe recalled the animals he'd met. Renaldo the fox and Streak and the monkeys. Were they genetic experiments, then? Had the scientists simply abandoned the project? If they had, they surely couldn't have realized what forces they'd left lying dormant in the place. And why had they left the monkeys? Joe wondered where the monkeys were now. Had they died or had they somehow escaped?

'Judy!' he called.

Hannah stood up, too. 'Come on, then,' she said. 'We have to go to my old house.'

'The cottage?'

'That's right,' Hannah said. 'It's over the hill. I used to live there with my mum. This way.'

'I know,' Joe said. 'I've been there.'

'You have?' Hannah said excitedly.

'Yes, we found it after we saw you being captured. But why have we got to go there? Can't we go home now?'

'It won't take long,' Hannah said. 'There's just one thing you have to help me with.'

'So you keep saying,' Joe said. 'But what is it that's so important for you to go back?'

'You'll see,' Hannah said mysteriously.

*

They were standing in the garden behind the cottage. It had started to rain. They were looking at the iron top that covered the well.

'I lived here with both my parents,' Hannah said. 'Dad was a scientist. He worked at the base, but he would never talk about what they were doing there. We were a happy family. I had friends here. It was like a little community. Then things started going wrong. There was an accident and some scientists died. And there were mysterious illnesses. Mum started getting worried and asking questions. She didn't tell me anything, but I could tell something was up. Then she and Dad started rowing.'

Joe thought of his own parents. They had been arguing a lot lately, too. Parents were like that. They never told you what was going on.

'Then my father died. It was awful.'

Hannah became quiet, obviously thinking of the ordeal she had been through.

'When was that?' Joe asked.

'Oh . . . a year or so ago. Then mum said we were moving. But on the day before we moved two things happened.' Hannah became quiet again.

'What were they?' Joe prompted.

'Firstly, my mother told me about some of the things the scientists had been doing. She wasn't going to tell me it all, she said, because it was too disturbing. But she'd been collecting information about it. After my father died some men had come and taken away all his files, but my mum had already made copies of a lot of the stuff. She was going to take it all to the newspapers and television. She said what the scientists were doing was evil and dangerous.'

'I think she was right,' Joe said.

'Then the second thing happened. They came and took us both away. We were bundled into a helicopter one night and that was . . . that was the last time I saw my mum.' Hannah's eyes were filling with tears.

Joe put his arm around her. 'What happened then?'

'I went to foster-parents. They said that mum would be coming back soon, but she never did. After a couple of months my new parents tried to find out where she was, but nobody knew. They said that the department had closed down. Everything they tried came to a dead end.'

'Didn't you tell them what had been going on?'

'Of course I did,' Hannah said. 'But no one believed me. Not even my new parents. They said I was being hysterical. Then they suddenly lost interest in trying to find my mother. They changed all of a sudden. It was awful. That's when I knew I had to come back.'

'But why? What was the point?'

'Because my mother had made a second copy of everything. She hid it here, in the well. She said that if anything happened to her, I was to come back and get it and take it to one of the big newspapers. She made me promise not to tell anyone about it. I came back but I couldn't lift the cover. So I realized I had to get help. Then I met you.'

'You mean that you brought me here, that I had to go through all that, the creepers and the rats, just because you couldn't lift the cover of the well?'

'Silly, isn't it?'

Joe stared at her, at a loss for words. Then he smiled and then he laughed. 'Silly isn't the word.'

Joe bent down and grabbed the old iron handle. 'Let's open it,' he said.

He heaved but it wouldn't budge. Together the two of them pulled. At last it came open. They pushed the heavy lid to one side. A thin rope was attached to a rusty nail. Hannah pulled the rope up. There it was. A package, wrapped tightly in a black plastic sack.

'Thank goodness,' Hannah said. 'It's safe.'

'I think you'd better give it to me,' Joe said. He took off his rucksack and hid the package beneath his sleeping-bag. 'I'll look after it. Just in case.'

'What do you mean?'

'We don't know that we can trust your foster-parents, do we? When you get back you might be searched.'

'But what if they search you?' Hannah asked.

'Why should they? I'm nothing to do with any of this. And if we go back separately, they won't even know we met one another. We can arrange to meet somewhere and then decide what to do.'

'I suppose so,' Hannah said.

'Just trust me.'

Hannah laughed. 'OK.'

'Now, let's push the cover back. Then we can go home.'

Judy began barking. They both looked round in alarm. Judy was sniffing round the back door of the cottage.

'What is it?' Joe asked her.

*The monkeys. I can smell them. Yes, I can.*

Joe and Hannah rushed over to her.

'Look,' Hannah said. She bent down and picked something up It was a strip of red T-shirt. 'Recognize this?'

Joe breathed a sigh of relief. 'Streak's bandana. They're safe, then.'

'I wonder where they are?' Hannah mused.

'On their way to Africa,' Joe said, and they both laughed.

They were making their way back down the track from the laboratories when they spotted the helicopter. And the helicopter spotted them.

CHAPTER 26

# BOOK-ENDS

Joe opened his eyes. He looked around in panic. But there was his mother. She was smiling. Suddenly he felt warm and safe. He was in his bedroom. He eased himself up in the bed and looked around the room. It was his bedroom all right. He could smell the familiar smells. There were his precious books on the shelves. And there was Judy, curled up asleep by his dressing-table.

'Hello, Mum?' he said. 'Is Judy all right?'

His mother laughed softly. 'Judy's fine,' she said. 'She's been in the wars, though. She had some nasty bites, but the vet patched her up.'

The marsh. The creeper. Judy. His memories came flooding back. 'Can we keep her?'

'I was afraid you were going to ask that,' his mum said. 'Can we?'

'Yes, I suppose so. If no one else comes to claim her. She's been very good, I'll say that for her. She hasn't left your side. And she's house-trained.'

They could keep her. Joe breathed a sigh of relief.

'The marsh . . .' Joe started to say.

'Shhh . . .' his mum interrupted, reaching across and laying her hand on his brow. 'Let's talk about it later, shall we?'

'But there was a creeper and monkeys and a talking fox . . .'

'I know,' his mum said quietly.

'You do?' Joe was amazed.

'The doctors warned me. It will be all right. You're not to worry.'

Doctors? What did she mean?

'They said you must have eaten something – something poisonous. They said it was something that must have given you hallucinations.'

'Hallucinations?'

'Yes. You've been asleep for two days more or less. Ever since they found you. They said you must have been wandering around on the marsh all that time with nothing to eat or drink.' His mum bent over and kissed him. 'We were so worried,' she said. 'But you're safe now, that's the main thing.'

Had he imagined it then, the marsh and everything that had happened? No, he couldn't have. It *was* real.

'What about Hannah?' he asked. Surely he couldn't have imagined Hannah.

'She's safe. She's gone home. Her parents are bringing her round tomorrow to see you. You must have had quite an adventure.'

'Her parents?' Joe thought about that. 'She told me they were foster-parents.'

Joe's mother looked serious now. 'They are,' she said. 'Hannah's been through a lot, but her new parents seem very nice, very . . . caring. I've seen a lot of them over the past few days. Everyone's been looking for the two of you since you didn't come back from fishing. We thought you might have met up. Hannah went missing over a week ago. There have been rescue teams out . . . everything. They even dragged the lakes. We were so worried. We thought . . . we thought you might have been . . . that is . . .'

Joe's mother suddenly stopped talking, tears springing to her eyes. She leant forward and hugged her son. After a while she stopped and sat up again, wiping her eyes with a tissue. 'But you're safe now, that's the main thing.'

Then Joe remembered.

'Dad! Where's Dad?'

'Downstairs. I'll go and tell him you're awake.'

Joe breathed a sigh of relief. 'I was looking for him,' Joe said. 'I thought he'd disappeared on the marsh.'

Joe's mum started weeping again. 'No,' she said through the quiet tears. 'He's not missing, but . . .' She didn't finish the sentence. Instead she stood up. 'Let's talk about that tomorrow, shall we?' she said, wiping her eyes on the now wet tissue. 'I'll go and tell him to come up.'

'Tell me now,' Joe said.

'Well,' his mum said, her voice faltering. 'We've decided . . . that is, your dad has decided that he's going to live somewhere else. That's why he was away for so long. But please don't worry. You'll still see him lots.'

Joe stared at her. Dad was moving out? Why? He and mum always seemed so happy, even if they did row a lot. He couldn't believe it.

'He forgot about taking you fishing. He's ever so upset about it. Don't be cross. I'll get him.'

His mum began to sob again. He watched her go. She closed the door gently behind her. His mum and dad were going to split up? It had happened to lots of his friends but he never dreamed it would happen to him.

He stretched and sank back into the warmth and comfort of his bed. He wasn't sure how he felt. Relieved that the ordeal was over, that was for sure. But the creeper, the monkeys . . . had he really imagined all that? Surely not. But something had happened. Hannah was real. Judy was real, too. He thought back to how it had all begun. He remembered the giant moth that had bitten him before he'd gone out on to the marsh. That had been real. And it must have flown in from the marsh.

Joe pulled back his duvet and crept across the room. His room was really tidy. His mum must have done it while he'd been gone. All his books had been put away on his shelves. Now, which one was it? That was it – his *Illustrated Guide to Moths and Butterflies*. He pulled it down and opened it carefully.

Yes, there it was, at the back, where he'd put it, pressed between the book's covers. A giant death's head hawkmoth. So that had been real, then. And if that had been real . . . that meant . . .

'Here, Judy,' he called.

The dog opened her eyes and, catching sight of Joe, leapt to her feet. She bounded across the room, her tail wagging, and plonked her front paws on him. Joe laughed and threw his arms around her.

'Judy,' he said, 'you're a good girl. And we're safe now.'

Judy licked his face. But, Joe suddenly realized, she hadn't said anything.

'Judy,' he said, 'can you talk to me?'

Nothing. No familiar voice in his head. Perhaps he *had* imagined it after all. The moth didn't really prove anything. But it had all seemed so real. Was it all a hallucination? A hallucination caused by something he'd eaten on the marsh. He stroked Judy and hugged her again.

*Your mum seems nice.*

Joe squealed with pleasure and hugged her even harder.

*Is this civ . . . civ . . .*

'Civilization? Yes, it is.'

*I like it.*

Joe had a worrying thought. What if Judy started talking to his mum, or his dad? He couldn't imagine what might happen. Dogs just didn't communicate telepathically in the real world. They'd think they were going mad or they'd have Judy taken away . . . anything might happen.

'Have you talked to my mum?' Joe asked.

*Of course.*

Joe's heart sank.

'What happened? What did she say?'

*Nothing. She just ignored me. Took no notice. Jolly rude.*

Joe breathed a sigh of relief. 'Don't worry,' he said. 'I don't think she could hear you.' He and Hannah were obviously tuned-in in some way. Perhaps Judy could only talk to children.

'Dogs can't talk here,' Joe said. 'But you're a special dog. You can talk to me and Hannah. But let's keep it a secret, shall we?'

*Yes, a secret. Keep it a secret.*

What an adventure! And his father was safe. But where was he? Joe listened. He could hear his parents talking in

179

the room below. The talking stopped and he heard the familiar slow tread of his father coming up the stairs. Then he noticed his rucksack, stowed neatly on his bottom shelf. The documents. The proof. He'd forgotten all about the black plastic sack of documents.

He rushed over and pulled his sleeping-bag out. Bits of dried-up grass fell on to the carpet. Thank goodness his mum hadn't decided to wash it. And there was the package, safe and sound. Thank goodness. He took it out and stuffed his sleeping-bag back in the rucksack. Then he hurriedly brushed the bits of grass to one side, hoping they wouldn't be noticed. He slid the package under the bed and clambered back beneath the duvet. Hannah was coming to see him tomorrow, his mum had said. They could decide what to do with it then.

The door handle turned. The door opened.

'Hi, Dad,' Joe said.